HONESTLY
ELLIOTT

Also by Gillian McDunn

Caterpillar Summer
The Queen Bee and Me
These Unlucky Stars

HONESTLY ELLIOTT

GILLIAN McDUNN

BLOOMSBURY
CHILDREN'S BOOKS
NEW YORK LONDON OXFORD NEW DELHI SYDNEY

BLOOMSBURY CHILDREN'S BOOKS
Bloomsbury Publishing Inc., part of Bloomsbury Publishing Plc
1385 Broadway, New York, NY 10018

BLOOMSBURY, BLOOMSBURY CHILDREN'S BOOKS, and the Diana logo
are trademarks of Bloomsbury Publishing Plc

First published in the United States of America in March 2022
by Bloomsbury Children's Books

Bloomsbury books may be purchased for business or promotional use.
For information on bulk purchases please contact Macmillan Corporate and
Premium Sales Department at specialmarkets@macmillan.com

Library of Congress Cataloging-in-Publication Data
Names: McDunn, Gillian, author.
Title: Honestly Elliott / by Gillian McDunn.
Description: New York : Bloomsbury, 2022.
Summary: Struggling with ADHD, loneliness, and connecting with his divorced father who would
rather see him embrace sports instead of cooking, sixth-grader Elliott finds an unlikely friend in
popular, perfect Maribel when the two are paired in a school-wide contest.
Identifiers: LCCN 2021031845 (print) | LCCN 2021031846 (e-book)
ISBN 978-1-5476-0625-2 (hardcover) • ISBN 978-1-5476-0626-9 (e-book)
Subjects: CYAC: Friendship—Fiction. | Fathers and sons—Fiction. |
Divorce—Fiction. | Cooking—Fiction.
Classification: LCC PZ7.1.M43453 Ho 2022 (print) | LCC PZ7.1.M43453 (e-book) |
DDC [Fic]—dc23
LC record available at https://lccn.loc.gov/2021031845

Book design by Jeanette Levy
Typeset by Westchester Publishing Services
Printed and bound in the U.S.A.
2 4 6 8 10 9 7 5 3

To find out more about our authors and books visit
www.bloomsbury.com and sign up for our newsletters.

For Jon

HONESTLY ELLIOTT

PART ONE

Split-Down-the-Middle Pie

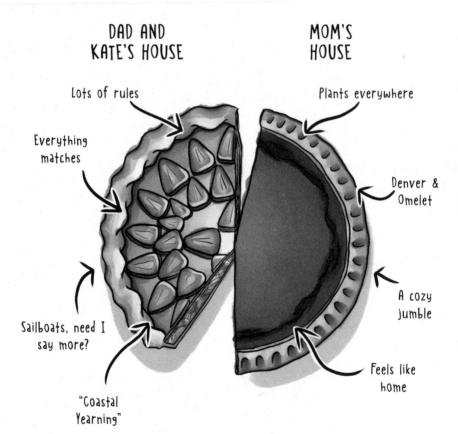

DAD AND
KATE'S HOUSE

MOM'S
HOUSE

Lots of rules

Plants everywhere

Everything
matches

Denver &
Omelet

Sailboats, need I
say more?

A cozy
jumble

Feels like
home

"Coastal
Yearning"

CHAPTER 1

If you saw me in the kitchen, you would think that I'm the kind of person who has it all together.

That's because cooking is my secret power. It's my favorite thing to do. And it also happens to be the place where I am most completely myself.

In the kitchen, I'm not my regular old always-late, homework-forgetting, not-many-friends, extra-disorganized self. When I become Chef Elliott, I'm focused. Confident. Decisive. I look at a pile of ingredients and see all the possibilities stretching out before me—everything that they can become—and I transform them into something bigger and better. When I start to cook, I'm calmed and energized at the same time. It's like a magnetic force I can't resist.

Which is probably why this Sunday afternoon—while Dad and Kate are out—I find myself poking around their kitchen. Even though it's maybe, technically, *a little bit* off limits. Which is unfair. But that's Dad and Kate for you.

A kitchen can tell you a lot about a person. Take Mom's, for instance—she lets me cook whatever I want. When I first got into cooking, she said, "I'm glad you have an interest in something, Elliott. But first I need to make sure you know how to be safe."

So I proved to her that I'm extremely careful when I cook. After she watched me long enough, she understood that I'm not going to set the house on fire or accidentally stab myself or cause a similar kind of catastrophe. Since then, I'm free to cook what I want when I'm there.

Mom's kitchen is the one I think of as *mine*. It's less than half the size of Dad and Kate's. The counters are old, and they're made of sunny yellow tile. The gas stove has a couple of burners that can be finicky, and the cupboards are crowded. But that kitchen is also warm and cozy. It's the place that feels like home.

The only thing about that kitchen is that I have to share it with a bunch of plants. The kitchen gets the best light in the house, and Mom has a giant green thumb, so we have at least a zillion[1] leafy green things hogging the counter at all times. If I complain, she says, "But, Elliott, have a heart.

---

[1] Possibly more.

This one needs just a bit more sunlight to get big and strong. You know that the closest thing to magic is when I get to watch something grow right in front of my eyes."

Inevitably, she gets all teary and reaches out to rumple my hair in this specific way that shows that means *me* growing too, not just her plants. I try not to roll my eyes because she's a good mom, even though she's mushy sometimes.

On Friday, before I left for Dad's, she showed me the latest addition.

Mom stared at the jar like it was made of rainbows and diamonds. "See, Elliott?"

I peered at the container. Most of Mom's plants are leafy or at least green. But this one wasn't either. It was just an avocado pit floating in water, suspended by toothpicks.

So that's what I said: "Mom, this is just an avocado pit floating in water, suspended by toothpicks."

She grinned. "Look closer."

When I squinted, I could barely glimpse the tiniest sprout that ever sprouted. Just a little white *nothing* pushing through the round brown seed.

Mom sighed. "This is it—this is the year I finally grow us our very own avocado tree."

I frowned. "It doesn't look like a tree. It doesn't look like much of anything."

Mom laughed, but she also pulled the jar close to her heart, like she was protecting it.

"Hush! You'll hurt her feelings."

My eyebrows popped up. *"Her?"*

She nodded, gently sliding the jar into a beam of sunshine. "Beth. Or maybe Imogene. I haven't decided."

So that's Mom. She's always been the type of person who sees the potential in things, and I guess I can't blame her for that.

Another main kitchen in my life is my best friend Malcolm's, which is right across the street from Mom's.

This is the story of me and Malcolm becoming best friends: a few years ago, The Divorce happened, and Mom said, "Elliott, we need a fresh start."

So Dad kept the house with the emerald-green lawn and the three-car garage and the neighborhood swimming pool with a water slide and giant diving board. Mom and I moved to our crooked little house in downtown Avery, where everything feels older and squished together but also more alive.

About ten seconds after the moving truck unloaded, Malcolm was on our porch, a basketball tucked under his arm.

"Hey," he said. "I'm Malcolm. Want to play?"

And that was it, easy as pie. It didn't take long for us to become best friends. Unlike a lot of kids, Malcolm never cared that I am terrible at sports. He would just shrug and say, "Don't worry, Elliott—it's no big deal. No one cares."

Maybe that was true at one point, but now that I'm in sixth grade it sure doesn't feel that way anymore. These days, when I goof up the other kids say, "Come on! Don't you ever pay attention?" And sometimes they call me Smelliott.

That never happened once when Malcolm was around. He's the kind of kid who's automatically good at everything—sports, school, drawing, you name it. That's another reason why I felt lucky to be his friend. I'm not good at everything. I'm not even good at *most* things. Especially sports. Especially school. And especially keeping my mind on one track.

The last part is because I have ADHD, otherwise known as attention deficit hyperactivity disorder. Otherwise known as: my brain is stubborn and likes to do its own thing. I think of it like this: Some people have regular brains—Dr. Gilmore says *neurotypical*. If you ask one of those brains to do something they probably say stuff like this: "Yes, absolutely! I would be happy to get that done for you on the double! Math equations? Fantastic! Paying attention to a little white ball, even though we're all the way out here in right field and no one hits it out here anyway? I'd love to!"

Yeah, that's not how my brain is.

If my brain isn't extremely interested in what's happening, it's like: *That's it, buddy! I'm out of here!*

Then it just stomps off down the hall or leaps out the window or dances around on a pogo stick instead of sticking with me.

One more thing about my brain—and this is the tricky part: even when I *really want* to stay focused, my brain sometimes takes off anyway. Sometimes I'm in a conversation and then I realize that I haven't heard anything the other person has said in the last ten minutes. It's like there's one Elliott who is there and listening and then there's another one who is off thinking about something that happened earlier that day, or planning a meal to make later, or noticing how sometimes clouds are fat and sometimes they're stretched out really thin and what makes that happen? Or, what if we lived in a world where dandelions were considered fancy flowers and roses were considered weeds?[2]

The only place that never happens to me is the kitchen. So you can understand why that's the right place to see me, if you want to know me at my best.

Okay, back to Malcolm's kitchen. His one mom Janice is an amazing cook, and she taught me a lot. How to hold a knife and the way to rock the blade in a smooth motion. Why everything should be cut around the same size so it all cooks evenly. How to taste, taste, taste at every step. Why any recipe that calls for a teensy amount of salt and doesn't tell you to add it in layers throughout the cooking process is basically a lie.

Their kitchen is on the older side, like Mom's, but with a smooth counter and heavy stainless steel cookware and

---

[2] Here's another one: Are hot dogs considered sandwiches? And another: Is water wet?

exceptionally sharp knives. Janice is the chef of the family, but his other mom, Grace, is a minimalist, so everything in their kitchen has to do more than one task. For example, no hard-boiled-egg slicers or cherry pitters, because you can do just as good of a job with a knife, which does both of those jobs plus a few thousand more.

Grace also believes in Tidying Up, so everything always has its very own place. Even the wok that's twice the size of my head. Even the smallest jars of expensive saffron threads and dried lime leaves and black cumin seed, tucked in the very back of the spice drawer.

I know that kitchen so well, I could cook there blindfolded—or I *could* anyway, if they still lived there. Last summer, Janice and Grace rented out their house. They bought an RV and are homeschooling Malcolm while they drive all around the country having adventures.

They were supposed to come back this summer. I'm not joking when I say I was counting the days. But last week, Malcolm sent me a postcard that said they're going to spend another year on the road.

Usually, I keep every single one of his postcards. Usually, I tape them to my wall.

But that one I crumpled up and threw in the recycling bin.

Best friends should never move away. Too many things have changed this year, or are about to change. Every single thing in my life has gotten worse since Malcolm left, if you really want to know the truth.

CHAPTER 2

Last year—right after Dad and Kate got married—the house projects began.

Kate likes things a certain way. First, she redid all the bathrooms even though they were perfectly fine. Then she painted every wall in the house. Before, they were just normal, but now the house has a color scheme she "borrowed" from one of the decorators she follows online. The rooms are painted Evening Leap, Gossamer Fog, and Coastal Yearning. They're all in-between-type colors: not quite beige, not quite gray, not quite eggshell. There's a reason they don't make a crayon called Coastal Yearning—can you imagine how much that would confuse a kindergartner?

The next project was changing our old deck into a screened-in porch.

Then she hung a monogrammed thing on the front door with her and Dad's initials. It's pink. Enough said.

She even decorated my room—which was supposed to be a surprise for my birthday. For the record, that is *not* a very good birthday surprise.

"Oh," I remember saying when she showed me. She stood there waiting, like she was expecting me to jump up and down with delight that my walls were now Whispered Wish and there were sailboats on every available surface. And I do mean *every* available surface. On my comforter. A big painting on the wall by my bed. Wooden sailboats on my bookshelves. And, unbelievably, a sailboat *trash can* next to my desk. As soon as I saw it, I wanted to throw that trash can right into the trash can, if you know what I mean.

Over my desk was another monogrammed thing, this time with my initials: *EQS*. I bet you don't know many people with a Q as an initial. That's a tradition in my dad's family—the firstborn kid always has Quigley for a middle name. It's the kind of thing that never comes up, but it's nice knowing it's there. It's like a secret handshake, or an invisible thread that ties Dad and me together. That part was actually okay.

But the rest of it? I just shook my head. Even though I know she worked hard on it. Even though I *know* it was supposed to be a special surprise.

Of course, I couldn't say any of that. All I could say was: "Oh."

Around the fourth time I said it, Kate's mouth turned down. Then she left the room kind of quickly. Her footsteps echoed as she went down the hall. The door to their bedroom clicked shut.

Dad sighed. "Honestly, Elliott—you should appreciate that Kate made an effort. She spent a lot of time on this."

Deep in my heart, I know that Kate is actually a nice person. That should make things better, but sometimes it makes it worse. Because maybe I need to be nicer. Maybe I need to do more. But I am trying, whether Dad and Kate see it or not.

I flopped on the bed, pushing aside a pillow that looked like a buoy. "I know she tried. But sailboats, Dad? I hate the ocean. I can barely swim!"

Dad made me apologize to Kate. I didn't mean to make her feel bad. But I also don't think I was wrong for wanting the one room in the house that was supposed to be mine to actually feel a little bit like me.

Kate's next project was the kitchen. This is one project I didn't mind one bit. Even now, months later, it still makes me catch my breath when I see it. It's the opposite of Mom's—there's nothing warm or wobbly or *old* happening here.

Walking into this room is like stepping onto the set of

one of those food channel kitchens. My favorite famous chef is Griffin Connor, who has his main show, *Cheftastic!*, along with six other spinoff-type shows—some are competitions, some are more travel related, some are kind of a mix of both. All of them feature Griffin Connor screaming at lots of different kinds of people. Some people think Griffin Connor is obnoxious—Mom can't stand the way he calls people Muffinheads and throws muffins at them.

"It's rude and disrespectful," she says. "And also a waste of food."

She doesn't understand that it's only because he wants everyone to do their best. There's a price to be paid for brilliance. (That's what Griffin Connor says anyway.)

Today the house is extra quiet because Dad and Kate are at their class. Usually they go Sunday evenings when I'm already dropped off at Mom's, but today they held it earlier for some reason.

I trace my hands over the cool marble countertops. Sleek and crisp, not a houseplant to be found. An enormous sink is set into the island. A separate, smaller prep sink is stationed near the fridge.

The best part of all is the professional range. It's twice as big as the old one and has eight burners with red dials. This is the type of stove that Griffin Connor uses on his show. It's much better than the stove at Mom's.

The whole kitchen is spotless. Gleaming. It's begging to be used.

And here's the part that really burns me up: no one ever uses it.

Okay, sometimes they make simple foods. I've seen Kate boil water for pasta. Occasionally, Dad makes pancakes. But otherwise, most everything is salads or takeout. It's a complete waste of those super hot burners. With them, I could get a better sear on meats. Sautéing would be a breeze. Don't even get me started about what it could do for my stir-frying.

Inside the refrigerator are mostly vegetables—lettuces, peppers, and cucumbers. Bottles of fat-free salad dressing. One package of boneless chicken breasts on the bottom shelf. A takeout container sits next to the peach-flavored sparkling water that Kate likes.

I move on to the walk-in pantry. Lots of basics—peanut butter, jelly, pickles, canned salmon, a jar of rice. There's a whole shelf of energy bars and protein shake stuff, which Dad got into around the time he met Kate. Before that, he was just regular-looking Dad. He had hair that was naturally messy, like mine, and he bought cheese puffs in those big plastic jars.

That Dad is long gone. Now he lifts weights and goes for runs and uses gel that makes his hair crunchy. The kitchen has been cheese-puff-free for at least a year. Maybe longer.

Lately, everything is so serious with Dad. Some of that is my fault, I know. I may have slightly messed up a couple of times this year. And by *slightly*, I mean even more than the regular, everyday kind of Elliott mess-up. I mean that I messed up in an exceptionally huge way. *Twice.*

A big mess-up at school—let's call that Almost Failing Sixth Grade. And a big mess-up here at Dad's, which I just think of as The Incident.

The Incident was a mess-up that topped every mess-up in the history of Elliott.

It is also why I had to start seeing Dr. Gilmore.

I do not like to talk about it.[3]

But it's not just because of the Almost Failing and the Incident. Some of what's changed is just Dad—the *new* Dad. The married-to-Kate Dad. The Elliott-better-shape-up Dad. The big-changes-are-coming-soon Dad.

The next shelf has a spice organizer. Most of the jars are still sealed, and the others are barely used. One by one, I examine them. Pink peppercorns, cumin, cinnamon, galangal—I wonder what made them buy that one, sesame seeds, poppy seeds—maybe Kate made muffins, I know she likes the lemon poppy-seed kind at the bakery, and dried basil,[4] yuck.

Then there's about six kinds of pasta. I pick up one of the boxes of the linguine, which reminds me of what Griffin Connor made on *Cheftastic!* last week—sesame noodles. They were rice noodles—not wheat like these, but they're

---

[3] Please don't ask.
[4] Dried basil is nowhere as good as fresh.

about the same size and shape. On the screen, they looked so good I could almost taste them.

The idea comes to me as I start to leave the pantry. I know they don't really want me to cook while they're gone. Honestly, they don't really want me to cook even when they're *here*. I tried once, and it was a disaster.

But Kate and Dad aren't here. Maybe I could make an entire meal for them. They'll be really surprised and happy not to have to cook dinner on Sunday night. I'll take some with me to Mom's and leave the rest for them. We won't be eating dinner in the same house, but we'll be eating the same food, so at least that's something.

I look back at the shelves. A familiar wave of calm washes over me. I know what I'm going to do, and it's going to be amazing.

CHAPTER 3

Confession: I am not the tidiest person.

Most people would know that just by looking at me. My shirt is always untucked. My hair is always messy.

Something not everyone knows: I may not be tidy, but before I cook I always triple-scrub my hands and up past my wrists almost to my elbows.

Then I wash my eyeglasses, which is something I never paid attention to until I started watching *Cheftastic!* For the competition shows, if someone arrives with smudged and crusty glasses, Griffin Connor throws them across the room. The *glasses*, not the contestant. But he has a reason—if someone's glasses are messy, you can't trust that their hands are clean.

One of my favorite parts of cooking is the moment just before it begins, when anything is possible. By the time I finish, my ingredients will be transformed into something entirely new. And I know that sometimes things might go a bit wrong. But, unlike the real world, most cooking mistakes can be fixed. The goal isn't perfection—the goal is making something new. Something delicious. Something that brings people together.

After drying my glasses on a striped kitchen towel, I switch on the music. I always need something playing when I cook—the louder, the better. If it's too quiet, it's impossible for me to think.

Okay. Now it's time to get started.

I look in a cabinet and find a bunch of little dishes with flowers on them. I'll use these for my mise en place, which is one of the first things Janice showed me. It means everything in its place. It means I do all my prep work—washing, chopping, and measuring—at the same time. Then the ingredients are ready when I need them.

After I wash the cucumbers, I peel them, making a big mound of their dark green skins. Then I scoop their seeds out into a pile next to the peels. I trim the bell peppers and heap their stems and membranes and seeds next to the peels. I'll sweep all of this into the trash later, but for now it is satisfying to see evidence of the work I've done so far.

Next up: chopping and dicing. I feel the rhythm of the rocking blade and watch the ingredients pile up: diced cucumber and onion, chopped garlic and ginger, a little pile of minced cilantro that I'll save for the very end. As I add the ingredients to the little bowls, I smell each one and imagine how cooking will change them. The onion's sweetness will develop, the cucumbers will become more flavorful, the soy sauce and chili flakes will blend with the peanut butter to make an explosion of flavor.

I don't use measuring cups—Griffin Connor is not big on measuring things. He actually says that in a meaner way. "Recipes are for losers" is the exact quote.

According to him, chefs have to develop an intuition about cooking. His cookbooks list ingredients but not instructions. Griffin Connor says *real* cooking is more about technique and inspiration.

In a kitchen, a brain that goes in six directions at once is actually an advantage. There's a lot going on, but it's never overwhelming.

Dad always says, "Elliott, if you can focus in the kitchen, then why can't you focus on your math homework?"

He thinks I'm faking it about the math homework. But he doesn't understand that cooking is my *thing*.

Math goes in a straight line. The answer is always the same.

That's not how cooking works. I'm keeping track of each part of the meal. I'm thinking about flavor and texture and if I cooked the protein enough. How else would I keep track of my skillet toasting the sesame seeds, the water coming up to boil, meanwhile whisking the thick sauce that will coat each and every noodle with peanut buttery perfection?

In math class, I have to sit still. My brain hates that.

But thankfully, a kitchen isn't like school. Here, I don't have to sit still. Here, I don't just listen—I get to touch the food, chop it, change it into something new. I get swept up in the bubbling-over energy, the constant activity. This is the place where my ADHD brain transforms into a super brain.

I'm serious about cooking—that's why I can't wait for this summer. Our town holds a four-week culinary academy camp, and this year I'm finally old enough to do it. In the morning we will shop at the farmers' market every day for fresh, in-season ingredients. In the afternoons, we'll go to real restaurants and get hands-on cooking lessons from professional chefs. In the final week of camp, we'll open our own pop-up restaurant and all the money raised goes to fight food insecurity here in Avery.

The experience, obviously, is priceless. The camp though . . . let's just say it's *pricey*. That's why I've been saving every bit of allowance and birthday money this entire year—and even with that, I still need some help from Mom, who said she'd pay half. That's meant a whole year of skipping slushies and sour straws at the movies, getting cookbooks only from the library, and watching a zillion annoying ads anytime I want to play one of the "free" video games on my phone. It has been a gigantic pain, but it's absolutely worth it.

You would think that simple fact would help Dad understand me better. But no matter how much I explain, he doesn't get it.

A few months ago—just before The Incident—I tried to cook for Dad and Kate, thinking that would help. It was a simple enough meal—steaks medium rare, a wedge salad, and a baked potato. I've made those same foods a hundred times when I'm at home. But that day was a totally different experience.

"Where are your knives?" I asked.

Kate rummaged in the silverware drawer. "How about this instead?"

I looked at what she was holding. It was a butter knife, the blade so smooth it couldn't slice an overcooked carrot.

When I was seasoning the meat, she said, "Isn't that a little too heavy on the salt?"

When I fried bacon for the salad, she said, "Maybe we should skip that part."

Not only that, the whole time I was in the kitchen, she didn't give me any space at all. She hovered around me anxiously, scrubbing at each tiny droplet I spilled until I thought she might wear a hole in the counter.

"Kate," I said. "I'll clean it up later."

But she just muttered something about stains and kept on sponging.

Finally, when we all sat down to eat, Kate ignored the salad because it had blue cheese in it, and then she thought the steak was too pink.[5] All she ate was the potato, and even then she really just nibbled at it. If I'm going to be honest, it wounded my soul. When I make food for someone, it's basically my heart right there on the plate.

The smell of the toasted sesame seeds pulls me out of my thoughts. I pour them into another flowered dish, and then I crank up the heat. I see every task laid out in front of me like stepping stones. First the chicken, then the veggies, and finally the noodles and sauce.

I add the chicken, and the oil spatters. It doesn't get on me—which is good, because I know that hurts—but it does get on the counter. The chicken needs my full attention, so I'll wipe up the mess later. Even on medium, this stove is a lot more powerful than Mom's.

After the chicken is browned on each side, I add the veggies. Meanwhile, I make the sauce. Peanut butter is hard to measure, and some of it glops out onto the counter. I taste every component as I go, seasoning as needed. Everything melds perfectly.

Just as I'm combining everything in a big bowl, the garage door whirs open. Dad and Kate are back from their class.

My heart jumps, imagining their happy expressions when they see that dinner is made. They're going to be so

---

[5] They were flawless.

22

excited. Kate's been really tired lately, so having dinner organized is going to be extra helpful. I already found a big plastic container so I can take some noodles to Mom and leave the rest for Dad and Kate to eat here.

But when they come in the kitchen, they do not look happy.

Dad draws in a sharp breath. His eyebrows arch sky-high.

I point to the giant bowl of noodles in front of me. "Look, I made dinner."

Kate's eyes go round. She takes in the counters with their piles and spills and glops. Her glance flickers to the used pots and pans on the stove. Her forehead wrinkles in a frown.

"I'll clean all that up," I explain. "Just wait until you taste this."

"Elliott," Dad starts, and then stops. Disappointment squeezes into each syllable.

El. You made a mess—again.

Li. You broke a rule—again.

Ott. You let me down—*again.*

My name hangs in the air like a cloud of steam. And that's when I realize that this isn't going to go like I imagined.[6]

---

[6] Not even close.

CHAPTER 4

They both start to talk at once.

Dad frowns. "You know you aren't supposed to use the kitchen when we aren't here."

"It's just for safety, Elliott," Kate says. "What if something caught on fire and no one was here to help you?"

I open my mouth and then snap it shut. I'm not going to start a fire! I'm very careful with safety.

My eyes start to tickle—I'm about to start crying. Some people cry only when they're sad, but for me it also happens when I'm angry or frustrated or generally upset. Whoever handed out Tear Tanks must have given me an extra small one. Whenever something bad happens, it's just a matter of time before it overflows.

I squeeze my arms around myself in a tight hug. "I was trying to help. Honestly."

Dad gathers the little flowered dishes from my mise en place and starts rinsing them in the sink. "These are antiques from Kate's great-grandmother. We don't ever use them."

My mouth drops open. "But they were right there in the cabinet. What's the point of having dishes that you aren't allowed to use?"

Kate, who has already started wiping up some of the spills, waves her hand like she's trying to brush away Dad's comment. "It's fine—you didn't know."

I grab a towel and dab a peanut butter smear. "I was going to clean after I finished."

Kate nods. "Unfortunately, stains set in pretty fast in the marble—and they can be permanent. I guess we never explained that."

When I'm stressed, I have this habit of rubbing my hand on top of my head even though it makes my hair stick up. I probably look like an overgrown dandelion right now.

"Sorry," I say. "I wanted to surprise you with dinner—"

I'm about to explain how I had the idea that they could have the same thing Mom and I will be eating. Even though we wouldn't all be together, we would be eating the same food.

Dad doesn't even look up—he's too busy brushing piles of my peelings into the bin. "We have plans tonight. One of my work associates and her husband are coming over for dinner. Now we have to clean the whole kitchen."

My insides feel like they're chopped, minced, and diced.

"I'm sorry." My voice cracks. I'm about to lose it.

Dad takes a deep breath. "It's okay, Elliott. Just get your stuff, it's almost time to go."

I race upstairs. When I open the door to my room, I groan and smack my forehead. It never fails. Every weekend at Dad and Kate's is the same: when I'm not looking, my backpack explodes its contents around the room. Sometimes I think my backpack is an evil entity that actively plots against me. Other times, I *know* it.

I begin my regular Sunday-afternoon scramble. This time, my heart beats faster than usual—if Dad sees this mess, he'll have another reason to be mad at me. That's the last thing I want.

First, I shove stacks of paper and piles of dirty clothes into the depths of my evil backpack. Then I push the mountain of books toward the bookshelf. I shuffle the papers on my desk into something resembling a stack. Before long, most of the Elliott-things are gone and the room is back to its normal, tasteful self. We wouldn't want the sailboats to have to look at a messy room all week.

I take a moment to look around. Not bad. What can I say, I work best under pressure.

"Come on, Elliott! Time to go!" Dad calls from downstairs.

"Two more seconds!" I shout back.

My graphic novel is wedged between my mattress and headboard. I grab it and stuff it into my bag. As I turn to go, my glance falls on the *EQS* letters on the wall. *Quigley* as a middle name, just like Dad. Today it doesn't feel like a secret handshake. Today it feels like it's the only thing in the entire universe that Dad and I have in common.

When I come back downstairs, Dad and Kate get quiet right away. I know exactly what that means—they were talking about me. The bowl of noodles sits on the counter.

"You can take that bowl with you—just bring it back next time you come over," Kate says.

I peek in the bowl. Some of the noodles are gone. I look at Kate in surprise.

She grins. "They looked really good, so I saved some to try later this week."

I smile back. Kate can actually be okay.

"They'll be even better if you add some freshly cut cilantro and toasted sesame seeds on top," I tell her.

"Will do," she says.

"Ready to go?" Dad asks.

I nod. Dad kisses Kate on the cheek. Together they stand, side by side, both with dark hair, tall, and athletic—almost as if, at any moment, they might decide to dash off to do a quick triathlon before dinner. Dad and Kate look *matching* somehow. I know Dad didn't ever look like that with Mom—she's shorter and softer and has blond hair and freckles, like me.

"We'll see you for dinner on Tuesday," Kate says. She lets her hand rest on her stomach.

I try not to look.

Because there is one obvious way that she and Dad are not matching. Not even a little bit.

The reason for this is coming soon—it's the reason everything is about to change.

A baby. The baby. *Their* baby.

Dad and Kate—and even *Mom*—say that the new baby will be my brother.

The truth is that it's one more thing that will never feel like mine.

CHAPTER 5

Dad's car smells like leather and lemon-fresh wipes. I hop into the front seat—and as I do so, I almost spill the jumble of noodles onto Dad's lap.

Dad has quick reflexes. His hand reaches out to steady the bowl. "Careful, Elliott."

Sighing and shaking his head, Dad reaches for his sunglasses, which are always in their flip-down compartment—exactly where they are supposed to be. Dad is not the type of person who misplaces his sunglasses.

The car is quiet as Dad backs out of the driveway, and I think—for once—that maybe we'll have a peaceful drive. Maybe we'll skip our regular father-son chat. But then he takes a deep breath and I know it's about to begin. My whole life, Dad's always liked to share his wisdom with me—I swear, sometimes it feels like he stepped out of one of those old television shows—the kind where dads know everything and all problems wrap up in less than thirty minutes.

But lately, these father-son talks have had a little extra intensity to them. Maybe because of the Epic Elliott Mess-ups. Maybe because of the baby coming soon—like Dad has to squeeze in all the father-son stuff now, because he's going to be too busy for me once his new son is born.

"Elliott," he says, and it's just like in the kitchen—I can hear all the disappointment and frustration, except this time it's unanswered questions that weigh those syllables down.

El. How come you almost failed the first half of sixth grade?

Li. Why don't you think things through?

Ott. Why can't you be more like me?

I push the button on the armrest, and the window glides down. I push another, and the seat moves forward with a quiet hum. Dad tenses up. He can't handle it when I mess around with things, especially *his* things.

He glances at me. "Quit fidgeting with the car."

He says it like there's a switch in my brain that I can turn off anytime I want. But it isn't like that for me. Sitting still is almost impossible—especially when I'm nervous.

"I can't help it," I say.

Part of me wants to add, "Be sure to include *fidgeting* on the list of all the things you don't like about me," but I manage to stop myself. Dr. Gilmore would call that *progress*. He likes to remind me that I can have thoughts without sharing them.[7]

"We need to talk about school," Dad says.

So it's going to be the talk about academics—the usual. More homework. More studying. More "accountability." Dad doesn't understand that school isn't for everyone. I'm not sure if it's for me.

As we get farther from Dad's subdivision, he keeps talking. I fix my glasses—which are sliding down my nose, like they always do—and then turn sideways to stare out the window. We always drive the same way from his house to Mom's. The roads get narrower and busier and more jumbled as we get closer to the heart of the city. Dad would say it's more chaotic, but in my opinion, it's more interesting. As we pass the park, I crane my neck for a glimpse of the playground with the rocket slide. Even though I'm too big for it, I still like knowing it's there.

Dad taps the steering wheel. "I checked the grade portal. It looks like you missed an assignment last week in math."

I wince just thinking of the expression on Mr. Gower's face.[8] "Okay. I'll make it up."

~~~~~~

[7] Dr. Gilmore is big on choices.
[8] I will take this opportunity to point out that *Gower* rhymes with *sour*.

Dad shakes his head. "You're a smart kid, but you need to apply yourself. Sixth grade is almost over. It's time to stop goofing around—soon enough, your grades will be part of your permanent record."

Sometimes when Dad talks, it's like a wall of information coming at me. The key is choosing the easiest statement to respond to.

"The school year isn't *almost over*. It's only April. Two more months to go."

He ignores me. "That's not the point, Elliott. You need to think about your future. When I was your age, I played four sports and got all As."

The thing about Dad is this: I know he's saying this stuff because he cares about me. But it's also not helpful to hear how perfect he was when he was my age. In fact, it's the opposite of helpful.

I slide down low in my seat. "School isn't easy for me. Sports are not my thing. You know that."

Dad drums his feelings on the steering wheel. For the first time since we got in the car, it feels like he's listening. He nods like he's thinking about my words. Maybe he's finally beginning to understand.

But then he sighs. "I worry, Elliott. You need to find a way to make connections with people—it doesn't have to be sports, but it has to be *something*. Ever since Malcolm moved away, you haven't done much of anything."

I scowl. "That's not fair—I do lots of things. I've been

working through the *Cheftastic!* videos one at a time. I'm learning a lot."

Dad shakes his head. "Not that silly cooking show again."

"*Cheftastic!* is not silly! Griffin Connor is the best chef in the world. No one can compare to his technique, his knife skills, the way he runs a kitchen."

Dad snorts. "I don't know about that. He throws things at people, Elliott. That's not exactly something to model yourself after."

I hug the bowl of noodles to my chest. "Griffin Connor has twelve huge houses with giant kitchens and enormous swimming pools and waterfall slides. He even has his own line of cookware. He seems to be doing just fine."

Now I've done it. Dad gets that look on his face, and I know what's coming. If Dad gave a TED talk, the title would be "A Celebrity Chef Is a One-in-a-Million Kind of Job." For an encore, he could also do "Elliott Needs to Get Serious about Math and Science." Or maybe he'd go with "When I Was Your Age, Here's Everything I Was Super Great At."

I clear my throat. "Dad, I get that you don't like Griffin Connor—that's fine. I learn from other people too. That's why I'm doing the culinary academy camp this summer—so I can get experience learning from actual chefs."

Dad's jaw tenses. "Right. Camp. I'm going to have to speak to your mom about that."

He launches into another long speech, but my brain has had enough. I barely catch the words *consequences* and *responsibility*, but the words slide over me. I find the loose thread on the hem of my shirt, and I wind it tight around my fingers.

I can tell Dad wishes he had a kid who was more like him, but he and I are completely different. He goes through life like a laser beam, in a line that's focused and direct. That's not how I am. My brain twists and turns like spaghetti noodles. Sometimes it gets stuck on an idea and stays there for a while. And I barely know the difference between a touchdown and a rebound.

Maybe that's what he'll get with the new baby—a son who matches him and Kate and their super focused, athletic, driven selves.

Maybe that's exactly what I'm afraid of.

We make a sharp left at a purple house and then pass Earl University, which is where Mom and Dad met.

Next, we circle the stadium for the Avery Crickets, with its baseball-hat-wearing cricket statue right out front. They're a minor-league team, and Dad always suggests that we go to games as a father-son outing. The last time he took me, I ate hot dogs and popcorn and jumbo sodas until I got sick. I don't think he would have minded that so much except I also let it slip that I had no idea which team was winning. Then I got an *Elliott* that said that Dad was extra disappointed that he had an indoorsy, nonsporting, sticky-spaghetti son like me.

When Dad pulls into the driveway, Mom's out front digging in a flower bed. A half-worn-out light bulb flickers in my brain. I was supposed to do the weeding before I went to Dad's, but I forgot. What else is new?

I get out of the car. Her eyes are crinkled up in a welcome-home smile. Mom knows I don't want a big fuss out here in the yard in front of the entire neighborhood—some things are off limits for sixth graders, especially sixth-grade boys—but we both know she'll give me a giant hug the second we're both inside.

"Hi, Elliott!" Mom's blond hair is tucked under her gardening hat, which has seen better days. She's wearing her too-big gardening overalls with mushrooms embroidered on the pocket. Compared to Kate, she looks like a little kid. Mom is not a makeup-at-all-times, shiny-earring-wearing, monogrammed-initials kind of person.

I show her the noodles in the bowl.

She beams. "They smell wonderful—can't wait to try them!"

Dad gets out of the car, stretching. Sometimes he stops to chat with Mom, and sometimes he doesn't. I know some people have divorced parents who can't stand each other, but my parents are mostly okay. They're nice—*too* nice. They prove it's possible to be friendly without being *friends*.

Mom brushes dirt from her knees. "Hello, Mark. I just remembered—I have something for you and Kate. Just a sec."

35

She disappears inside. Dad and I stand in the front yard. I shift the bowl of noodles from one arm to another. He peers at the roof like he's doing an inspection.

"One of those shingles is a bit loose," he says. "Might want to mention it to your mom."

Dad used to make lots of remarks about ways to improve the house until one day Mom told him we would manage just fine on our own. Now he makes those little comments to me, instead. He thinks I have extra responsibility as the man of the house. I don't know about that, but I do try to remember things like the shingles, which seem important.

When Mom returns, she holds a gift bag. It's light blue and has little ducks on it.

She hands the bag to Dad. "I was out shopping and couldn't resist."

I frown. "What is it?"

Mom's eyes crinkle. "It's for the baby, of course."

My throat tightens. Of course. The baby.

Dad smiles. "Thank you, Nina. That's nice of you."

"How's Kate feeling?" Mom asks. I grimace, looking at the dirt and the weeds I forgot to pull.

"Tired," Dad says. "You know how it is."

It's quiet for just a moment then, and I wonder if it's awkward for them. Of course Mom *knows how it is*—she knows from when she was pregnant with me. Now Dad's new wife is having a baby. Isn't that weird for everyone?

But Mom just says, "Yep! He'll be here before you know it."

I clench my hands into fists and then relax them. It's not because I want to punch something. Tensing up and then relaxing is a strategy from Dr. Gilmore. It's supposed to help me get down when I'm feeling overwhelmed. Today it doesn't work.

Mom looks at me carefully. She has that mom X-ray vision and can tell when I'm getting upset.

"Why don't you go put those noodles inside?"

She doesn't have to ask twice.

"'Bye, Dad," I say over my shoulder as I head up the steps to the front door, which I open with a crash. Inside, I drop my backpack on the floor. It's good to be home.

CHAPTER 6

Each time I come back from Dad and Kate's, I can't help but notice the difference between the two places. I may have two houses, but only one of them feels like home.

Here with Mom the house is warmer, busier. The wood floors slope a bit, but she says that just adds character. My bedroom walls are turquoise because that's my favorite color. The living room is the color of mandarin oranges, the kitchen is pea-pod green, the dining room we changed into a library has butter-colored walls with shelves stuffed full of books and two extremely comfy chairs. There are paintings on the wall, art posters, and even some vintage seed packets. There's a shadowbox displaying Mom's collection—the key to every house she's ever lived in. Nothing is themed. There are no sailboats. Everything feels real and one of a kind. This is where I fit best.

I'm greeted by a chorus of squeaking. It's my guinea pigs, Denver and Omelet, saying hello from their corner of the living room.[9]

"Hey, guys," I say. "Did you miss me when I was gone? Did Mom give you some lettuce to munch on? I'll be right back—just let me put away this food."

I got Denver and Omelet after The Divorce. I originally wanted a dog, but Mom had guinea pigs when she was a little girl and she talked me into them. Now I can't imagine what it would be like without these funny, cuddly little guys.

Denver's face is half-brown and half-white, split almost down the middle. He has one dark eye and one blue eye, which is rare. His hair sticks out in every direction, and he loves to run fast. Omelet is more relaxed, with a cream-colored smooth coat and huge brown eyes.

I head to the kitchen. On the wall is a big whiteboard that is part calendar and part to-do list. Most of Mom's list has to do with gardening and paying bills. My side has exciting[10] stuff like chores and homework. Squeezed in among the houseplants is a stack of mail, and right on the very top—*yes!*—is a postcard from Malcolm. It has a picture of a very strange-looking animal on one side.

---

[9] *Squeak, squeak, squeak!*
[10] By *exciting*, I really mean *painfully boring*.

Elliott,

This is a jackalope—part jackrabbit and part antelope. Supposedly, it's a mythical animal and they don't really exist. But I'll let you know if I find any. Do you think they taste like chicken? Ha ha.

Malcolm

I grin. He never writes all that much, but I can practically see his face and hear his voice saying the words.

I open the refrigerator to put the noodles inside. As soon as the door cracks open, Denver and Omelet start squeaking as loud as they can. They know that the refrigerator = fresh vegetables. I grab them a few carrot sticks and go back to say hello and give them some attention. They chomp on their snack and scurry around the cage.

After a while, I hear Dad start his car. The front door clicks shut, and Mom comes into the kitchen. She squeezes me in a giant hug.

"You're getting so tall—you're up to my eyebrows!" Mom says this kind of thing almost every time she hugs me, especially when I've been away at Dad's. She uses a half-happy, half-sad kind of voice, like part of her can't believe that I'm not a little kid anymore.[11]

"Come keep me company in the kitchen," she says. "After all that gardening, I could use some water."

[11] I know I'm not supposed to admit this, but sometimes I can't believe it either.

I follow her. She gets two big glasses from the cabinet and fills them both.

She takes a long sip. "Whew! It was hotter out there than I realized. How was your weekend?"

I shrug. "The usual. Dad tried to get me to go for a run, and I said no. Then he tried to throw a football with me, and I said no to that too."

Mom sighs. "He's trying to find common ground—trying to connect with you."

"Then I actually tried to do something nice. I made dinner while they were at their baby class. But no, that made them mad too," I say, frowning into my water glass.

Mom raises an eyebrow. "He mentioned that they were surprised when you made the noodles. Were they mad about it? Or were they a little disappointed and frustrated about having to deal with a mess?"

This sounds like something Dr. Gilmore would say. Sometimes my brain jumps immediately to thinking the worst about things. But remembering the disaster of this afternoon makes the Tear Tank threaten to overflow. "I *do* try. That's why I made the noodles."

Mom leans over and pats my arm, smiling in a way that looks a little sad. "I can't wait to try them. Let's eat."

I pull out two bowls and dish the sesame noodles into them. They are delicious—and sticky—just like Griffin Connor said they would be. I explain to Mom how I made them with peanut butter, and she seems impressed.

Mom twists them around her fork and takes a big bite. "These are incredible!"

"Thanks," I say. "I was wondering if they needed a little lime juice or something to brighten them up."

Mom shrugs. "They're great just as they are."

We're quiet for a while, eating. Mom always appreciates my food. But still, sometimes I wish that I got to cook for a big group. When Malcolm lived across the street, his family always had Lost-and-Found Thanksgiving. They invited all their friends and the friends of their friends. Anyone who wanted had a spot at their table. There was always enough to go around. I miss that feeling.

Mom twirls some noodles on her fork. "Earlier, Dad stayed because he wanted to talk about—*you know*."

Her words jolt me out of my thoughts. I know what she's talking about, all right. The Incident. I hate thinking about it. I pick at a piece of cilantro left on my plate.

She sighs. "Dad says he wants you to pay him back for the damages."

My face gets hot. *Damages*. Something about that word is uncomfortably official. "But I was already grounded."

Mom shakes her head. "That was a punishment. Think of this as more of a consequence."

My eyes get wet. That Tear Tank again. It's embarrassing sometimes, the way my feelings leak out.

"Elliott?" Mom says. "Did you hear me?"

The food, which was delicious a few moments ago, has

now turned to a flavorless lump in my mouth. I swallow hard. "All right. How much is it?"

"Six hundred dollars," Mom says.

I must have heard wrong. My eyes get big. "*What?*"

"Six hundred dollars," she says again, sounding a little less patient this time.

I twist my napkin in my hand. "For a *window*? That's ridiculous. Where am I supposed to get that kind of money?"

She pauses, and in a rush, I know exactly what she's going to say. I gasp, I actually *gasp* like I would have if a zombie strolled into our kitchen, taken away our noodles, and instead served us up a big heaping pile of fresh brains. I cannot *believe* that Dad would do this to me. There's no way. It's impossible, even for Dad.

"Mom. *No!*"

She tilts her head sideways. "You *do* have the money saved, Elliott."

My eyes are so wide, I can feel them bulging out. "That's for culinary camp! I've been saving all year!"

"Is it fair, though, for you to do that camp instead of paying him back?" Mom asks.

I start to answer, but she shakes her head.

"Wait," Mom says quietly. "Think before you answer."

I squeeze my eyes shut. I did epically mess up, I admit that. But this seems so unfair.

"Do I really have to give up camp? It's not like Dad needs the money," I say.

Mom folds her napkin. "I don't think it's about that. It's more that he wants you to understand that your actions have consequences. As your parents, it's our responsibility to get you ready for the real world—Dad and I both take that seriously."

I shake my head. "But *you* would never make me give up camp because of something like this."

Mom tilts her head. "Dad and I might handle things differently, but you'll also have teachers, coaches—and even, one day, bosses at work—who do things differently too. Think of Griffin Connor. He has his rules for his kitchen, right? And this consequence is a *lot* more reasonable than the muffin throwing and screaming that Griffin Connor does."

I sink back in my chair. For once, the Tear Tank seems to be empty. I must be in shock. I'd rather get hit by a thousand muffins than give up camp.

Most of the time, I try really hard not to think about The Incident. But here's a question: Have you ever tried *not* to think of something? The classic example is elephants. Okay, right now, whatever you do—don't think about elephants. Go on. I'll wait right here.

Waiting.

Still waiting. Remember, whatever you do, no elephants, okay?

That's what I thought. You're thinking about elephants, right? It's because you can't not-think of something without thinking about that thing.

It's the same for me and The Incident. Whenever my brain dances over in the general direction of The Incident, I push it away as fast as I can. But if I'm being honest, that means I actually think about it all the time.

Maybe if I paid Dad back, I wouldn't feel that way anymore. And maybe Dad wouldn't be so disappointed in me.

Mom is still looking at me, her question hanging in the air. *Is it fair to go to camp instead of paying Dad back?*

"I know I should pay him back," I say haltingly. It's like the words stick in my throat. "But I don't want to give up camp. What if I find another way to earn the money?"

Mom hesitates. I know what she's thinking—it's taken me a whole year to save up. How could I earn the money in such a short time?

"I suppose you could see if Dad and Kate might pay you for doing yardwork and other chores. Or even helping with the baby," she says.

The idea of spending extra time with the baby is enough to make me shudder. "Ugh. No way."

Mom sets down her fork. "I'm sorry, Elliott. I know this camp means a lot to you. Maybe next year."

My insides feel heavy, like a hunk of overcooked oatmeal. Meanwhile, my brain starts going in six hundred directions. Six hundred things blocking my way to culinary camp. Six hundred reasons for Dad to be disappointed in me.

I have to think of something.

PART TWO

Monday-Morning Pie

PIECRUST:
lattice crust—plenty
of holes for things
to fall through

FILLING:
green tomatoes & underripe bananas—
because no one's ever ready for a
Monday morning

CHAPTER 7

Whoever invented Monday mornings should be fired.

"Elliott!" Mom's voice echoes from the kitchen. "Breakfast!"

"Be right there!" I shout.

It's mostly true. I'll be there soon. Right after I locate a pair of socks.

Unfortunately, this is harder than it sounds, mostly because of Thursday Elliott. Thursday Elliott forgot to check the whiteboard in the kitchen, where purple letters announce Elliott—Laundry.

Which means Thursday Elliott didn't *do* laundry.

Which also means Monday Elliott has no clean socks.[12]

---

[12] Maybe Thursday Elliott is the one who should be fired.

Don't panic, I tell myself. Dr. Gilmore would like that. He is big on positive self-talk. When something goes wrong, I'm supposed to say things to myself like *It will be okay—I will find my socks eventually*. But some days, positive self-talk feels a lot like lying.

I swivel my head, taking in the room. Bookshelves, closet, a messy bed. One wall where I tape Malcolm's postcards. As usual, my desk is covered with piles of books and papers. I have to admit that most of the floor is covered too. In the corner, the hamper overflows. I'm not necessarily above rewearing a pair of lightly used socks, so I shove the laundry mountain sideways to make it topple over.

A single mud-crusted sock appears—that must have happened that time I wore socks outside in the garden, which Mom always tells me not to do. Besides the mud, the sock smells strongly of cheese, which I don't even want to spend time thinking about.

I drop it on the floor and kick the rest of the laundry around—no luck. I've heard Mom make jokes about where all my socks go and how the dryer must eat them. Ha ha.[13] But now I'm wondering if that's a real thing. Like maybe our dryer has a portal to another land—one where they have so many extra socks they could never ever wear them all.

I sink to the floor. Even in my room, I can smell the breakfast Mom's cooking—the eggs, potato, salsa, and turkey

[13] Total Mom joke.

50

sausage. She cooks three things better than I do: grilled cheese, tomato soup, and breakfast burritos. No matter what I try, they don't turn out like hers. My stomach grumbles. If it weren't for Thursday Elliott, I'd be eating right now.

Underneath my nightstand, the corner of a big book pokes out. It's *Cheftastic! Cooks for a Crowd: Making Food That Matters*. Malcolm sent it to me for my birthday. When I unwrapped the package, my insides crumpled. He probably doesn't realize that my only hope of cooking for a crowd vanished when he and his moms left.

But even though I felt a few pangs when I first paged through, I couldn't help but read it anyway. After all, it is a cookbook—a *Griffin Connor* cookbook—and soon enough, I was drawn in by the super close-up glossy photography, the pages of cooking techniques, and, of course, the list of Muffinheads' Dos and Don'ts.

I pull the book out, and it cracks open to my favorite page—the one with beef Wellington, which is supposed to be one of the most challenging dishes of all time. I've watched the video on the *Cheftastic!* website enough that I know the steps almost by heart. I sit down and look at them anyway, recreating the dish in my mind.

Looking at the beef Wellington reminds me of stuffed mushrooms, which I was thinking about just the other day. I flip through to find it. The pictures are so vivid, they make my mouth water as I imagine the combination of acidic, salty, and buttery flavors. Then I turn the page, stopping to study the picture of seafood soup. I can picture it bubbling away, steaming up the kitchen windows on a chilly afternoon. I'd serve it with crusty bread and herbed butter.

"Elliott?"

I freeze. In my head, I could almost taste the food. In real life, Mom is standing in the doorway. She does *not* look happy.

Casually, I slide the book underneath my bed. I try for a smile. "Hi, Mom. I'm almost ready—just looking for some socks."

Mom gives me a sharp look. "In a cookbook? Nice try."

My cheeks flush. "I was just . . . checking something."

Mom frowns. "You said you'd be right there. That was fifteen minutes ago. Mornings are busy enough—I need to be able to count on you."

I frown. "I'm sorry, okay? But it was just one extra minute."

Mom checks her phone. "More like twenty."

My jaw drops. That's impossible—there's no way I lost track of that much time. But the clock on my nightstand doesn't lie. 8:02 a.m. I need to get to the bus, or I'm going to be late.

I jump to my feet. "I got sidetracked."

"Hurry, Elliott. You're going to miss the bus, and I can't be late today," she says.

The words make me freeze. Mom never loses her patience. But today she actually sounds irritated with me.

"I'm really sorry," I say. My voice scratches.

Mom takes a deep breath. She types into her phone, probably texting her boss. If Mom is late to work, she might get in trouble. Maybe she would even lose her job. Then it would be all my fault. My face feels hot.

"I'm *sorry*," I say again. The Tear Tank is about to spill over.

Mom shoves her phone in her pocket. When she speaks, her voice is light and calm, like usual. "New plan: No bus. Let's just find the socks, and then I'll take you to school. Did you check the laundry basket?"

My throat squeezes. Now I *really* feel like I'm going to cry. The socks. The laundry. That's what got me into this mess. I look down at the floor.

"I forgot to do laundry," I mumble. And with that, the Tear Tank finally overflows. I scrub at my eyes, trying to push them away.

I feel embarrassed. I'm also mad at myself. I wish I didn't need help with things. I wish I could remember everything I'm supposed to do. Dr. Gilmore says this is part of the challenges with ADHD—that feeling this way is normal. That's why we have systems, like writing things down. But that doesn't help if I don't remember to check the whiteboard.

In another universe, maybe there's a version of me who does everything right the first time and never gets distracted. Maybe in that portal universe with all the extra socks there is a Thursday Elliott who remembers to do his laundry, then folds everything and puts it away.

I ball my hands into fists and press them against my eyes, pushing my glasses up on my forehead. I want my tears to go away. I want this whole *day* to go away.

"Hey," Mom says softly. "El. Are you feeling overwhelmed?"

I force myself to nod.

"Let's take some deep breaths," she says.

It takes a while, but eventually I feel more settled.

Mom squeezes my hand. "I'm sorry I was short with you. Our whiteboard system is making a difference, but we should also make sure we do check-ins. I'll try to remind you about that."

"Okay," I say. "But what about my socks?"

She smiles. "Be right back . . ."

Mom disappears into her room across the hall and comes back holding a pair of her socks. "These ones okay? We're about the same shoe size now."

I reach for them. Mom always wears the weirdest socks, and these are no exception. They're orange and have grinning koalas. Normally I wouldn't be caught dead in them, but today I don't have much of a choice. *Don't cry.*

"Your shoes are by the door," she says, like she can anticipate what I need to hear next. "Go get them on and I'll wrap up your burrito. Okay?"

"Okay," I say.

I hurry to get ready, trying to push aside the worries about being late and about making Mom late for her job. I go say hi to Denver and Omelet. They need fresh water and more of their guinea pig food. I stick my hands in their cage and feel their soft fur. My heartbeat slows and my breath steadies. Eventually the spiky prickles of panic smooth enough that I can breathe.

In the car, Mom hands me the burrito. It's still hot, even through the foil.

"Thanks, Mom," I say. "And—sorry. About the socks. And for being late."

Mom shrugs. "It happens. We're okay."

Mom is very good at looking on the bright side of things.

I unwrap one end and take a giant bite of burrito. I close my eyes as the tastes and textures fill my mouth. Salty sausage, creamy eggs, crispy potatoes, and a hint of acidity from the salsa. It is the ultimate breakfast.

When I open my eyes, Mom is smiling at me.

"I think I made it a bit too big," she says.

I shake my head. "Impossible! There's no such thing as a too-big breakfast burrito. Especially yours."

She laughs. "You don't need to flatter me."

I grin. "Just being honest. I can't help it that my mom makes the most amazing burritos in the universe."

Mom swats my arm in a joking kind of way. "Okay, that's enough!"

I settle against my seat. Mom's car is a beat-up hatch-back she's had since before I was born. It's not all that clean either—I see an empty salad container in the back seat, and the trunk is stuffed full of donations that she's been meaning to drop off at the women's shelter.

But I don't mind a little clutter. In Mom's car I feel about a million times more comfortable than I ever will in Dad's lemon-fresh luxury vehicle.

If I weren't wearing orange koala socks, I could almost forget that the awful morning ever happened. That's just how it is with Mom and me.

CHAPTER 8

The morning is cool and crisp and bright. Mom drives us through the streets of downtown Avery, which are lined with all kinds of restaurants. The fancy ones don't serve breakfast on weekdays, but they have delivery trucks coming and going, mostly from local farms.

Until I got into cooking, I never really understood the concept of a fruit or vegetable being *in season*. I mean, the big grocery store usually has pretty much everything you could think of. But while you could technically buy a watermelon in January, it probably wouldn't be all that good—and it probably was grown pretty far away. Lots of people have heard of *eating the rainbow*—eating fruits and vegetables in lots of different colors so you get different vitamins and stuff. Not everyone knows that you can eat the calendar too—around here, that means peas, broccoli, and cabbage in spring; zucchini, eggplant, and okra in summer; pumpkins, sweet potato, and squash in fall.

Mom gets a red light in front of Sugar Rose, where the line for doughnuts is out the door. They're expensive, so it's not something Mom and I get very often. They are tasty though. There are all kinds of people in line. Young and old, tall and short, different skin colors and races and nationalities, and probably speaking different languages. The diversity is part of why Mom wanted to live near downtown, and I like that too.

Two people in business suits come out, holding big boxes with the Sugar Rose logo on top. A group of college students follow, each holding a doughnut in one hand and coffee in the other. I spy several Sugar Rose doughnuts—their signature item, which is frosted with pale pink icing, then covered with candied rose petals and the lightest, fluffiest spun-sugar cotton candy. It may sound weird, but the combination of textures and flavors is out of this world.

Mom nods at the line. "Someday, that will be you."

"Waiting in line for a doughnut?" I grin. "Yeah, probably. Hopefully someday *soon*, hint-hint."

Mom laughs. "No, silly. I mean people lining up for *your* food. Someday."

Mom knows that's my dream. Some days I see it so clearly that I can even imagine the font on the menus. Other days—like today—it's impossible to imagine how I could ever get there.

"Maybe," I say. "We'll see."

"If that's what you want, it will happen," she says firmly. "And I'll be first in line."

"Not for doughnuts though," I say quickly. Griffin Connor isn't a big believer in bakeries and sweets. He says it's not a real kind of cooking.

Mom raises her eyebrows. "Too good for doughnuts? I'll remember that the next time you ask for a trip to Sugar Rose."

"Not too good to *eat* doughnuts," I say. "But I'd never *make* them. Griffin Connor says that pastries and baked goods appeal to the masses. It's not the same as *real* cooking. No one's palate was ever elevated by eating a doughnut sugar-bomb."

Mom tilts her head sideways. "As always, Griffin Connor sounds like he could stand to be taken down a notch."

I frown. "*Mom!* Griffin Connor knows what he's talking about."

Mom frowns, tapping her fingers on the steering wheel. "I think it's tricky to talk about *real* cooking. After all, doughnuts are real to the people who make them—and eat them. Sugar Rose is doing good business, and that's real too."

I gulp my burrito. "But, Mom—"

Mom shakes her head slowly. "I don't like the idea of being negative about what other people like. What makes him the authority? Why is *baking* somehow less important than cooking?"

I wipe my mouth. "Because he's a genius, that's why. A literal genius."

She opens her mouth like she's going to say something else, but then she just sighs. "I know you're a fan, Elliott. But sometimes it's good to think about these things a bit deeper."

"I do think about them," I say. I can hear the stubbornness in my voice.

Mom reaches out and pats my arm. "Okay, great. That's all I ask."

The light turns green, and she steps on the gas. I consider what she says. But I also happen to believe that Griffin Connor is right. He says cooking is about inspiration and baking is about control. Basically the difference between art and science. Bakers are stuck on boring old recipes and fiddly things like getting measurements exactly right. Griffin Connor says that's not what being a chef is about. Cooking should be about magic, and fire, and dazzle. Not measuring a teaspoon of this and a tablespoon of that. That's the kind of thing a Muffinhead would do—not even a Thursday Elliott would do that. Not now, not ever.

CHAPTER 9

We pull into the circle in front of Avery Sixth Grade Center, which everyone calls ASG for short. Our car inches forward in the drop-off line.

Mom gazes upward. "I'll never get tired of looking at this building."

"I know a couple thousand sixth graders who would disagree," I say, but I'm mostly joking. Even though school isn't my favorite place, I can admit that the building is really cool and impressive with its outer walls made entirely of glass. Four stories high, each level has sleek technology centers and squashy couches for coworking spaces. Everyone in our town considers it the centerpiece of the Avery School System.

"I don't know," Mom says. "My middle school didn't look anything like this."

I finish my last bite of burrito and wipe my mouth. "It's far from perfect, Mom."

Mom looks at me sideways. "I thought you liked it."

I shrug. "It's huge-normous.[14] Even now I still get lost sometimes."

Mom laughs. She probably thinks I'm kidding. I wish I were. Last week I walked into the wrong classroom—without even realizing it, I was on the completely wrong floor. Everyone laughed, and I heard at least one kid fake-cough *Smelliott*. Fake-cough talking should be outlawed.

"The school has to be big so it can fit all the sixth graders in Avery," she answers.

Like lots of cities, Avery has lots of schools scattered all over town—newer suburban schools on the outside of town and smaller, older schools in the city center. There are elementary schools and middle schools and high schools. But for one single year—sixth grade—every kid in Avery goes to ASG, which is located right smack in the middle of the city. The idea is to provide a unified experience for everyone—so no matter what elementary we went to and what high schools we will all scatter out to, at least we have this one year with everyone together in the same place.

"Besides, it's beautiful," Mom says, in that relentlessly

---

[14] What do you mean, that's not a word? It should be!

optimistic way she has. "You do the most interesting projects. Plus, the Avery Local stuff is so cool."

Avery Local is the theme of the school. It's painted on our walls in splashy colors and typed on every parent newsletter. But it's not just a slogan—everything we learn ties back to the city of Avery in some way. So when we studied civil rights, we had a partnership with the senior center. They shared their memories of the segregated schools that existed right here in Avery and helped everyone understand how wrong that was. When we did a unit on chemistry, we had actual demonstrations from Earl University students. Sometimes we even get special lunches brought in from local restaurants—those days are my favorite.

Another part of ASG is that it is project based. Each quarter we rotate through different units and projects. These projects are a big percentage of our grades. You could say that's part of the reason I almost failed first semester.

"Sometimes I think it would be easier if I went somewhere smaller," I say. "A place where I actually knew more of the kids."

Mom looks at me sympathetically. I had a really hard time when school started. Even though I knew there would be a Malcolm-shaped hole in my life, I expected to know a few kids from my elementary school in some of my classes. But through some scheduling quirk, I got put with kids I didn't know.

"The point is," she says, always positive, "you made friends. Think about lunch. You didn't know anyone at the beginning of the year. Now you have your little group that sits together every day. Drew, Victor, Kunal, and—"

"Gilbert," I say. "They're okay."

She smiles her sunshine, see-everything-is-fine kind of smile.

It's true that I've made some friends. It's also true that they are just *okay*. Even though I eat lunch with them, we haven't really crossed over from school friends into real-life friends. No one ever talks about how hard that can be.

It would be easier if we had more in common. They all love soccer, and I don't. They all play *Kingdom of Krull*, but Mom and Dad don't want me playing video games they consider violent—even though there isn't even any blood in *Kingdom of Krull!* So when they want to talk about the game, I don't have anything to add. Sometimes I watch gamer videos on YouTube just so I can understand what they're talking about.

It's not just video games though. Every so often I have the sneaking feeling that they hang out without me. Maybe it's my fault. Sometimes I space out when people are talking. Other times, I might blurt out my ideas and interrupt someone. I know it's just because I'm afraid I'll forget what I wanted to say. But sometimes when I do it, I see the other kids exchanging glances. Maybe they think I can't control myself. Maybe they think I'm being rude.

Back in elementary, this wasn't a big deal. But sixth grade is different. Some people have social media accounts with thousands of followers. And some people are even *dating*, which is beyond weird to me. It's like I keep waiting for someone to stand up and say, "Hey, did everyone forget that we are still basically kids?" But no one ever says that, of course. So maybe it's just me who feels that way.

Before long, Mom's car reaches the front of the line. I get out and sling my backpack over my shoulder. In an absolute miracle, I have exactly ninety seconds until the bell rings.

"Have a good day!" Mom calls as she drives away.

She says it as if good days come easy. They don't—not for me anyway. My stomach tightens as I think back on the morning. It would be hard to think of a worse start to the day. And here I stand with koalas on my socks, which is awkward at best and social-outcast at worst.

My throat tightens, and my eyes twitch like they're going to fill with tears.

But. I have a mom who gave me those socks. And who made a burrito for me. And who gave me a ride to school so I wouldn't be late.

When I think about it, my problems this morning were all because of Thursday Elliott. It seems like Monday Elliott might have a decent chance at a good day after all.

CHAPTER 10

My first class is Advisory, which meets twice a week. We don't usually learn actual things in here, just do projects and hear announcements and stuff like that. This is where I met Drew, Kunal, Gilbert, and Victor—they're all in this class too. So I'm glad for that—otherwise, I'd be eating lunch by myself every day.

The teacher is Ms. Choi. She has spiky hair and wears in-line skates on what she calls Roll-In Wednesdays. None of the students are allowed to wear them—but it's still pretty cool to see her skating around the classroom.

The bell rings right as I walk in the door.

I scramble for my seat. Sitting in the front row is supposed to minimize my distractions. In reality, it means that the front row of the classroom is full of the other kids who get distracted. The super smart kids sit in the middle, and the popular kids sit in the back.

Ms. Choi walks from row to row, handing out stapled packets of yellow papers. I got to know her pretty well this year when the first big Elliott mess-up happened—the Almost Failing First Semester thing.

The thing that no one told me is that sixth grade is different from elementary school. At my old school, I had one teacher to keep track of. One set of papers. One set of assignments.

Now that I have lots of classes, there are about a gazillion things I'm supposed to organize. Specifically, there's a lot of paper. So much so that it was slightly overwhelming. And by *slightly*, I really mean a huge, epic amount of overwhelm.

I slowly stopped doing my schoolwork—instead, I stuffed the unfinished work into the corner of my closet. A few pages at first, then more. Then, eventually, all of them.

Then I started putting my scribbled-red-ink test papers in the pile, too. Because I figured, hey, those homework handouts were probably a bit lonely.

Next, I reached the big time. It turns out that those stapled packets explaining the projects also explained that they were a huge part of my grade. Who knew? Not me. Because, yeah, those papers ended up joining the homework and test papers. And I sort of, definitely, skipped doing a few[15] projects.

Mom and Dad were so mad when they found out I hadn't been doing my work. It turns out that there's this grade portal thingie for keeping parents informed, but there was a typo in Mom's email address and they didn't have Dad's. So things escalated a little further than they should have. Now they are on that portal like hawks on innocent field mice.

The one good thing about those meetings was Ms. Choi. She's actually the reason I didn't fail. She's the one who reached out to my parents and attended every conference—ones with the counselor and assistant principal with scary words like *Retention* and *Summer School.*

But Ms. Choi was nice about it. She said we needed to come up with a structured plan for me. That I needed more support. And she was right. I ended up making up the work, even though it practically killed me. Every time I turned in something, she looked me right in the eye and said, "I knew you could do it, Elliott."

Never underestimate the power of one person believing in you.

So I guess it's obvious that I'm actually a real live fan of Ms. Choi, even though it's not the kind of thing I could ever admit out loud.

"We've got a lot to cover today, so let's get started."

---

[15] All of them.

Ms. Choi is laid back, but she's still a teacher. Slowly, everyone stops chatting and turns their focus to her.

"Today we're starting our local business projects," she says. "The packet has the information you'll need, and we'll also go over it in class. Remember, you can always come see me if you need extra help. We're in this together."

She catches my eye and makes a goofy face for a fraction of a second—a secret signal, to remind me that she's there if I need her. Of course I just look at my paper and pretend not to notice.

"With this project, you will create a business plan and be given a budget. You'll then execute your idea at our Avery Local festival next month," she says.

For a project, this one is actually okay. Mom and I go to Avery Local every year. There's lots of craft items and foods and some quirky little invention-type things. One year, back when I was little, I even got a superhero cape with my name spelled out in silver iron-on letters.

"As you know, the entire community is invited," Ms. Choi continues. "From your booth you can demonstrate a prototype of your idea. Or, if you choose to, you can sell items and keep the profits."

I sit up straighter. In all my years of going to the festival, I had no idea that the kids selling things got to keep the money they made.

And then it hits me: Maybe, if I come up with the right item to sell, I'll be able to pay back Dad. I could go to culinary camp!

"This project is the culmination of everything you've learned at ASG," she continues. "We expect you to challenge yourselves. Remember, if you don't prepare you will be standing at your booth for the entire four hours with nothing to show for it. It's worth planning ahead."

She pauses. "Unlike our other units this year, there is only one project. This means that your project grade counts for fifty percent of your grade in all your core classes."

Gulp. I'm bad at math, but even I know that is a *lot* of grade resting on a single project.

"Oh, and another thing," she says. "This is a *group* project. You can have anywhere between two and five people in a group. Not one. Not six. Due to space constraints, there is absolutely no flexibility on this rule, I'm afraid."

I turn sideways, deciding that waving down Gilbert is my best bet. He sits three rows behind me, in between Drew and Kunal and right in front of Victor—smack in the middle of smart kid city.

"Gilbert," I whisper. "*Gilbert.*" But he doesn't look in my direction.

Ahalya, who is also part of smart kid city, raises her hand. "Ms. Choi? On page eight it says we need to make a poster for the final project. Can we do an interactive slideshow instead?"

I shake my head. Sometimes these smart kids really are like laser beams. We've barely even gotten the assignment, so I haven't even thought about specific details. All I care about is finding a group.

I lean sideways in my chair until I'm almost hanging all the way out of it. "Gilbert," I whisper. He looks at me. I point to myself and then to him, moving my hand in a kind of a circle to include Drew, Victor, and Kunal.[16] Gilbert looks away quickly like he doesn't understand what I'm asking.

"Hang on, everyone," Ms. Choi says.

She's crossed the room to stand by my desk. I slide back into my seat and look forward, hoping nobody notices that my face is turning red. I've seen my school plan, where *proximity* is recommended as a nonverbal redirection strategy. Really, that's just a teacher way of saying that sometimes I get back on task if a teacher stands by my desk. It has the added benefit of them not having to say *Elliott* all day long. Which, let's face it, some people say more nicely than others.

"We're going to have some time now to find your groups and do some preliminary brainstorming. The project is due next month, so you'll be moving at a quick pace. By the end of this week, you should have your proposal submitted, so use your time wisely."

My insides feel like a smoothie in a blender. All I can think of is needing to talk to my lunch friends. I try to send them my thoughts: *I want to work with you guys.* My knee bounces as I attempt to ignore the tornado in my stomach. Waiting is agony.

Ms. Choi smiles. "Let's remember to keep the volume to a dull roar. Go ahead."

---

[16] This is the universal sign for *Hey, I want to work with you guys.*

The second the words are out of her mouth, I leap out of my seat and squeeze through the row to Gilbert. I lose my balance and have to grab the top of his desk to keep from doing a face-plant on the floor.

"*CanIworkwithyouguys?*" The words come out in a rush.

Gilbert hesitates. "Um, I think the four of us are going to work together."

"The four of you?" I glance at Victor, Kunal, and Drew. "But it's five to a group."

"Five to a group *maximum*," says Drew. "Not minimum. We aren't required to have five."

It feels like a cartoon where I can see the words hanging in the air—but even though I can see them, they don't sink in all the way. I stand there, blinking.

Drew squints at me. "I think we have different work styles."

"No offense," says Victor. "But you are not the easiest person to work with in a group."

"Oh," I say, finally getting it. They don't want to work with me. The twisting and turning in my stomach turns into a giant knot.

"Hang on," Kunal says. "Maybe we can make a space for Elliott."

Gilbert shoots Kunal a dirty look. "You know we already decided last night on the group chat."

I frown. "What group chat?"

Kunal's eyes widen. There's a long pause where no one says anything.

And then I realize that I'm right—that I was right all along. They *do* hang out without me. They even have their own group chat without me. They probably talk about me all the time.

"*Anyway*," says Victor. "Like I said, no offense. We can still have lunch together and everything. But fifty percent of a grade is a lot."

The other guys nod like it's settled. "No offense," they all say, even Kunal.

The thing about *no offense* is that it's always said immediately after someone says something totally offensive. Think about it. If you say something nice, you would never in a gazillion years think to add on the end "no offense." That's because no one ever needs to say *no offense* when they say something nice. Those words are basically an announcement that whatever just happened was completely mean.

"Okay," I say. "Okay. No big deal."

My voice shakes. My eyes are suddenly wet. *No big deal* is a lie. But if I cry right now, it will become an even bigger deal—an epically humiliating deal. I've cried at school before, but I've always been able to make it to the bathroom stall before the Tear Tank overflows. So I just squeeze my hands together and try not to blink.

I walk back to the front of the class. I need to find another group. But as I look around everyone[17] is already talking with their groups. Ms. Choi may have been joking when she

---

[17] Absolutely everyone.

requested a dull roar, but it somehow feels exactly like I'm walking through a wind tunnel. I sit at my desk, not sure what to do.

Ms. Choi sees me sit and comes over. "Elliott? Do you need a group?" Her eyebrows pinch, making a line in her forehead.

I swallow. I'm afraid if I nod, the Tear Tank will really overflow. It will be like a dam bursting.

Her eyes glance at the Victor-and-Gilbert huddle. "What about—"

I shake my head back and forth fast. "They don't want to work with me."

Her eyebrows pop up, and then a look of understanding crosses her face.

"It's okay," she says soothingly. For the first time, I realize that *It's okay* is like a cousin to *No offense*. Most people only say it when things are pretty far from okay.

Ms. Choi frowns, studying the room. "It's okay," she says again, almost like she's trying to convince herself. "We just need to find you a group to fit in with."

My cheeks get warm. I don't want her to force a group to take me. "No," I say firmly. "I'll figure it out myself. I'm just—uh—just going to sharpen my pencil."

I grab a pencil off my desk and walk to the corner table. My pencil is sharp enough, but I need to pretend to do something while I look around the room.

Ahalya is sitting with three girls and drawing something

on graph paper. Nate and Alex are twins, and they always work together. It must be nice to have a built-in group partner. Xavier and a bunch of the popular boys are huddled together—if Victor and those guys didn't want me, those other guys would flat-out laugh if I tried to join them. Besides, there's five of them already and Ms. Choi said no exceptions.

And then there's the group of girls who sit in the back—they're so popular they're practically famous. For some reason, I always think of those girls with their first and last names together. Kennedy Eubanks. Pranathi Chari. Claire Jennings. Parker Kobayashi. Maribel Martinez, who is not only popular but also has the best grades in our entire class.

They're all sitting together, like I would expect. But it sounds like they're disagreeing about something.

"No way," says Kennedy. "That would be super gross."

Parker rolls her eyes. Maribel bites her lip, looking at Kennedy carefully. Then she looks down at her desk, rummaging in her binder. She picks up a pencil and heads toward the sharpener—toward *me*.

I freeze.

When she gets closer, I can see that she looks upset. Her cheeks are red, and she's holding her eyes open wide, like she's trying really hard not to—

Wait. No.

Maybe?

—Like she's trying really hard not to cry.

Maribel Martinez? With an almost-overflowing Tear Tank? Impossible. But that holding-eyes-wide-open is the oldest trick in the book. I'd know it anywhere.

I finish grinding my pencil to a nub and step to the side.

"Thanks, Elliott," she says.

Oh. Okay. I had no idea she even knew my name. I try to make my face look totally normal.

"Are you all right?" I talk kind of out of the corner of my mouth, I'm not sure why.

"Not really," she says grimly. "My group is terrible."

"I thought they were your friends," I say.

Maribel shrugs. "I thought so too."

I glance at Victor and those guys. I know exactly what she means.

Maribel finishes sharpening and inspects the tip of the pencil. She must decide it is sufficiently pointy, because she turns to go.

Here's one thing I wonder about a lot: Do most people think about what they're going to say before the words come out? And if so, how much—is the entire sentence formed inside their head? Or is it like it is for me, when the slightest spark of an idea can mean a whole bunch of words tumbling out like they have a mind of their own?

"Wait," I say. "Maribel? Do you want to work with me?"

CHAPTER 11

As soon as the words are out, I regret them. If I could, I'd cram them back in my mouth. But it's too late.

Maribel turns back, her eyebrows raised. She looks at me like she's seeing me for the first time.

I have no idea what she's thinking—she's probably about to say, "In what universe would I, Maribel Martinez, ever work with messy, disorganized Elliott?"

Or maybe she's thinking she better head back to Parker and those other girls fast.

Or maybe she's about to say, "Oh, you thought I called you Elliott? You must have misheard me—I actually called you *Smell*iott."

But she doesn't say any of that. Instead she asks, "What are those?"

She's squinting at my ankles, so I look down. Right. Mom's socks. My cheeks get hot.

"Koalas," I mumble.

She's quiet for a moment. Then she says something I never would have expected, not in a gazillion years.

Maribel Martinez looks right at me, and she says, "Okay. I'll work with you."

Before I can pinch myself, before I can say, "Are you *sure?*"—before I can even make a peep—Maribel heads back to her desk. She leans over to talk to the girls she sits with, and one of them glances over at me.

I put the pieces together. She was joking. Of course she wasn't really going to work with me. And now she's telling the other girls all about it.

My ears flame red. They're so hot, someone could probably fry an egg on them.[18] I hurry back to my desk, where the project packet is sitting, untouched. On the first sheet we're supposed to list the members of the group we're working in. My page is, obviously, blank.

"Okay, people," Ms. Choi says. "I need to know who everyone is working with. Take that top sheet and pass it to the front—one per group."

In a flash, I see my future: Another project packet crammed in the corner of my closet and my grades for this

---

[18] Except that would be an extremely unsanitary thing to do. Griffin Connor would not approve.

semester will plummet. I'll have to use my culinary camp money to pay back Dad. And then I'll either enroll in summer school or repeat sixth grade on an endless loop, or possibly both. Malcolm will come back and move on to seventh like everyone else, and I'll have to stay behind.

Ms. Choi stops by my desk. "Elliott? Do you have a paper?"

My heart is beating fast. My insides are squishy like overripe bananas. I open my mouth, but no sound comes out.

Ms. Choi stands there, waiting.

And of course, my good old buddy the Tear Tank is standing by as usual. This time it's almost as if I can hear it talking to me, and *wow* does it have a lot to say.

Good morning, everybody, Tear Tank says in a sportsannouncer kind of voice. *We're here to witness an astounding display of the most powerful waterworks known throughout the land, brought to you by the one and only Elliott . . . Quigley . . . Sawyer!*

[A light smattering of applause comes from the crowd.]

It's a record-breaking kind of Monday, folks, and we're glad to have you here at Ms. Choi's Advisory period! We're about to join together in a very special countdown as we see if Elliott can actually dissolve in a puddle right here in front of the entire class. That's right, folks, if all goes as expected we are about to see the first example of human liquification!

[The crowd goes wild.]

Let me hear you say three . . .

Let me hear you say two . . .

Let me hear you say—

"Elliott," someone says. And it's Maribel, sliding into the desk next to me.

I look over at her. She's holding a spiral notebook and a clear pencil case that has tons of colorful pens inside, but right now she's holding the pencil she just sharpened. The project packet rests on top of her notebook.

"How many *L*s and how many *T*s?" she says.

I tilt my head sideways. "What?"

She taps her pencil impatiently. "Your name. I'm trying to write it, but I don't know how to spell it."

It takes me a moment to put it together. This is happening. Maribel *does* actually want to work with me. She's trying to write our names on the project paper. Although, the longer I take to answer, the more she looks like she's wondering if being my project partner is a very good idea.

"Two of each," I finally manage to squeak out.

Maribel writes my name—with perfect penmanship, I might add—and makes a flourish underneath. Then she hands the paper to Ms. Choi, who takes it with a smile.

"What an interesting pairing," Ms. Choi says. "I can't wait to see what the two of you come up with."

Ms. Choi moves along to the next desk. Something pokes me in the elbow.

"Come up with a lot of ideas so we can talk about them next time," Maribel says. "Because we're going to get an A on this project."

I want to tell her to adjust her expectations. I've never gotten an A on anything this entire year, and I've certainly never gotten anything approaching an A on these big projects.

But the bell rings, and Maribel disappears on the way out the door. Something tells me she's never late to class.

The good news is that I didn't fall apart when Victor told me I couldn't work with them. The good news is that I actually found someone to work with on this project. The good news is that I did it without crying.

The bad news? Now I'm working with someone who won't settle for anything less than perfection. And, as everyone knows, perfection is not exactly my specialty.

This is either the best thing that's ever happened to me or the worst thing that's ever happened to me—I guess I'm going to find out which.

CHAPTER 12

Sometimes a day starts bad and ends up being good.

Sometimes a day starts bad, gets a tiny bit better, but ends up cascading into awfulness.

Guess which day I'm having?

In gym, we play pickleball, which I hate. I'm not very fast, and I'm also not very good at hitting a ball. If Malcolm were here, at least we'd have each other. He's so good at sports that it makes up for my lack of skills. But Malcolm is cruising in his RV, hiking at the Grand Canyon, or checking out the world's largest ball of aluminum foil. So gym is terrible, as always.

Math—realized I left my homework at Dad's. Mr. Gower gave me a short-tempered *Elliott* when I told him that. Mr. Gower is not my favorite.

Language Arts—listened to more information about our business project. We're going to have to make a slideshow, poster, and four-page document just for the proposal. That's just to get approval—that's not even the final project! I am trying very hard not to think about it.

Lunch—I sit with Gilbert, Kunal, Drew, and Victor because I don't know what else to do. They don't say "no offense" at any point, so that's good. But the entire time they talk about their school project. Victor has the idea to make *Kingdom of Krull* catapults out of wooden craft sticks. Which, honestly, sounds amazing.

Gilbert turns to me at one point. "Are you and Maribel working together?"

I crumple my chip bag. "Yeah."

Kunal wrinkles his forehead. "How did that happen?"

I shrug. I would tell him if I understood it myself.

"She's super smart," says Drew. "You'll get the easiest A ever."

I guess that's supposed to make me feel better, but it just makes me mad.

I clench my hands. "You say that like I'm going to let her do all the work."

Gilbert shifts in his seat. Victor and Drew exchange glances.

Kunal hesitates, but then nods. "You wouldn't do that."

Victor holds up a sharing-size bag of Skittles. "Who wants some of these?"

We all take a handful. Everyone else shoves the entire handful in their mouths at once, but I eat them one by one.

They go back to their discussion about leverage and rubber bands. I look around the cafeteria. Maribel is sitting with Parker Kobayashi and those girls. For the fiftieth time so far today, I wonder why she isn't working with them.

After the school bus drops me off, I go inside and go straight to Denver and Omelet's cage. They make their happy welcome-home squeaks. I take them with me to the kitchen and block off the exits so they can run around without escaping. It's only fair that they get some exercise when I'm doing my homework.

I drop my backpack on the kitchen floor and grab a bowl of leftover sesame noodles from the fridge. Not to brag, but they taste even better today. Sometimes the most important ingredient for any recipe is a little patience.

Denver scurries from one side of the kitchen to the other. Little Omelet sniffs at my feet. I pat the soft fur on his back, and he makes low purring sounds. Guinea pigs are really good communicators. No one gives them credit for this.

I glance at the whiteboard. Homework, it says in lime-green letters.

Right.

When I was little someone read me that picture book about the mouse who wants a cookie but there's about a hundred things the mouse gets reminded of so he starts doing those things instead. It basically takes him the entire book to finally get the cookie. This is basically what my life is like, except usually there's no snack at the end.

I unzip my backpack, looking for my math paper. But I can't help keeping an eye on my guinea pigs. They have such different personalities. Denver travels all over the kitchen, running back and forth like he's having himself a little jog. Omelet likes to hang out closer to me.

"How was your day?" I ask. He sniffs my foot in response. I guess guinea pigs' days are pretty much always the same.

"Mine was terrible overall," I tell him. I explain about Advisory and the huge project. How Maribel is somehow my partner and how it feels knowing I'll let her down. Of course, Omelet can't understand me, but somehow it makes me feel better when he looks at me with his big brown eyes.

I dig down to the bottom of my backpack and find the math worksheet crumpled into a ball. I smooth out the big wrinkles and start the first problem. Then I remember that the weekend's homework is still at Dad's. My stomach folds in on itself. Mr. Gower is going to be mad if I don't have it tomorrow. And Dad's definitely going to check that parent portal for missing assignments.

I pick up my phone, planning to text Dad about the homework. But instead of pressing his contact, my finger freezes in place, hovering over his contact photo, which is a picture of the two of us from last year's father-son Crickets game outing.[19] Dad won't be home until tonight. Plus, he will make me feel bad for forgetting it in the first place.

I swipe backward to the directory and scroll to Kate's name. She has an office in their house and mostly works from home. Before I can think too much about it, I press her name and the phone starts ringing.

"Elliott? Is everything okay?"

She sounds worried. I don't remember the last time I called her. Maybe I never have before. Usually I just talk to Dad.

"Yeah," I say. "Um. How were the noodles?"

"Oh!" Her voice brightens. I can almost imagine her leaning back in her chair. She's probably wearing a sweater, because Kate is always cold. "They were delicious! I had them for lunch. I was going to save some for your dad, but I couldn't stop eating them—they were that good!"

I smile. "I'm glad."

Then we're both quiet for a moment. Her fingers click the computer keyboard. She's probably in the middle of something important. I'm about to say goodbye, but then I hear her voice again.

"Elliott? Are you sure everything's okay?"

"Actually," I say. "It's been a bad day, kind of."

The clicking stops. "Oh," she says. "I'm sorry."

She says it with just the right amount of niceness. Not like she feels sorry for me, but like she cares.

---

[19] Taken before I barfed, of course.

Have you ever had a terrible day?[20] One rotten thing happens, and then another. Eventually, it starts to feel like a whole pile of awful is stacked on top of you. But the weird thing is that if someone comes along and is nice to you, that's the exact instant you suddenly start crying.

Or if you're me, you start sobbing.

I hold the phone away from my face so Kate can't hear. It takes a while for my tears to stop. I wipe my face on my shirt and blow my nose on a paper towel.

"I'm sorry," I tell her finally. "I was calling because I left my math homework there. I think it's on the desk in my room."

"Should your dad take it with him tomorrow? He's picking you up after your appointment with Dr. Gilmore," she says.

I shake my head, even though she can't see me. "That's after school. I need it in the morning."

"No problem," she says. "I'll scan it and text it to you. You can print it out or maybe email it to your teacher."

"Thanks, Kate."

"Of course," she says.

I don't want to start crying again, so I just say goodbye and hang up fast.

---

[20] Not just a little bit bad—I mean really horrible.

CHAPTER 13

Every Tuesday afternoon, I am supposed to walk straight to Dr. Gilmore's office, which is seven blocks away from school.

I eat a granola bar on my way, and I look in all the shop windows. There's a store that only sells soap—I got Mom one there that smells just like a chocolate bar. There's Avery Market, a specialty grocery store that sells all kinds of unusual local things, like pickled peaches and weird mustards and olives. I love looking around there and finding new things to taste. Lucky me also made friends with some of the cheese counter people and they always save little odd-sized pieces for me to sample.

Then I make a left on Case Avenue and go two blocks

onto Flory. Dr. Gilmore's office is a big house that was converted into a therapy practice. It's a huge building with lots of windows and turrets, and it's painted the soft orange of a papaya, with creamy yellow trim.

I go up the wooden steps and through the front door. The waiting room has a bunch of random furniture in it, antiques that someone reupholstered in some of the strangest patterns—like an armchair with fried eggs and waffles, throw pillows with octopuses, and a sofa that looks like a strawberry. Somehow it all works together.

Ms. Jolene, the woman at the front desk, smiles when she sees me. "Elliott, go ahead and grab a seat. Dr. Gilmore will be ready for you in just a minute."

"Okay," I say. I grab a peppermint from her candy bowl and take it with me to the elephant armchair.

Dr. Gilmore isn't the first therapist I've seen. Back in elementary school, when I was first diagnosed with ADHD, I saw someone named Mrs. Susan. We played with clay a lot. She made suggestions for how to make school and home a little easier for me, like the to-do list on the kitchen whiteboard. But Dr. Gilmore is the kind of therapist who talks about feelings.

After a few minutes, Dr. Gilmore shows up. He has curly hair on top that's shaved close to his head around the sides, bright white teeth, and glasses, just like me. He's really tall and skinny and has ears that stick out, which I think gives him a friendly look.

He comes over to where I'm sitting. "Ready?"

I follow him through the hallway, where we have to be quiet so we don't disturb other kids having appointments with *their* therapists. We walk past sound machines that make shushing sounds, which I guess is so everyone has privacy.

Inside his office is a big yellow sofa—which is where I usually sit, a blue chair—which is where Dr. Gilmore usually sits, and a striped rug. On the wall behind the blue chair, the words *Mad, Sad, Brave, Calm* are painted.

On the wall behind me is a big painting of the ocean. Once, I asked Dr. Gilmore about it, and he said that looking at the sea makes him feel peaceful. I don't think of the ocean like that—I don't like how big it is. It feels wild and unpredictable. The only thing I can think of that makes me feel calm like that is cooking, but people don't usually hang pictures of kitchens on their walls.

I drop my backpack with a *thunk* and flop onto the sofa.

Dr. Gilmore nods at the bookshelf. "Do you want to pick something out?"

When I started going to therapy, I didn't know what it would be like. I definitely didn't expect games. But Mom explained that sometimes games are a good way to help people feel relaxed—especially kids.

I ignore the blocks and art supplies and pick a card game with animals dressed like pirates.

Dr. Gilmore shuffles the deck while he explains. It's sort of like UNO, but there are a bunch of rule cards with different variations and you pick different rules to play with each time. Sometimes walruses are wild cards, and sometimes you have to draw an extra card if you play a rabbit— stuff like that. It seems like a good pick because the rules in my life seem like they're always changing too.

After we've played for a while, he asks me about my week.

I place a penguin card on top of a turtle. I'm still thinking about Maribel and feeling worried about the project. But it's not the main thing on my mind.

"You know how I saved up all that money for culinary camp?" I ask.

Dr. Gilmore nods. He plays a card on top of mine.

I put down another card. "Dad wants me to use it to pay him back for The Incident. It's six hundred dollars."

Dr. Gilmore nods slowly. "What do you think about that?"

I rub the hair on top of my head. "I think it's unfair in one way. It's my money. Going to camp is important to me."

"It *is* a lot of money," Dr. Gilmore says. He's quiet for a moment. "You know, Elliott, we've never talked about what happened that day. Maybe we should."

For some reason, I can't get comfortable—I scoot backward in my seat, then sit sideways, then tuck my legs up underneath me. Mom calls it "ants in your pants," which is kind of gross but also a good way to explain that itchy, wiggly kind of feeling that makes it feel like I can't sit still.

"I bet you already know," I say. "My parents probably told you."

He shrugs. "I'd like to hear it from you."

I toss my cards on the table. "I'm not going to talk about it. I *hate* talking about it."

Dr. Gilmore calmly plays a card with a turtle and a tiger. "Have you ever heard of mountains and molehills?"

I wrinkle my forehead. "That's an old saying, right? 'Don't make a mountain out of a molehill.' It means that you shouldn't change something small into something big."

Dr. Gilmore nods. "It's something you might want to think about, Elliott. I know you don't like to talk about what happened. But calling it The Incident and refusing to talk about it might be making this bigger in your head than it actually is."

The back of my neck feels hot. "I don't think that's true. It's big in my head because it actually *is* big."

Dr. Gilmore's face is calm. I don't mean this in a rude way, but he looks kind of like a turtle himself right now. Nothing bothers turtles. They're unflappable.

I, on the other hand, am extremely flappable. I'm not sure that's a word, but it should be. I stand up from my chair and go look out the window.

"People make mistakes, Elliott. It's part of being human."

I wince. The image of the basement window pops into my head. The sound of glass cracking. The kicked-over bucket of baseballs at my feet. Dad's face when he saw what

I had done. Most people don't make *that* kind of mistake. Even I know that.

I glance at the digital clock on Dr. Gilmore's desk. "Our time is almost up."

We finish our game, and Dr. Gilmore stacks the cards neatly in the box. He walks me to the lobby. Dad's not there, but I can see him through the window, standing on the front steps. He's on the phone—probably a work call.

"'Bye, Dr. Gilmore," I say.

He looks at me seriously. "Mountains and molehills, Elliott. Think about that this week."

"Okay," I say. But I already know that I won't. The Incident isn't a molehill, and it isn't a mountain. It's the worst thing I've ever done. I don't want to talk about it or even think about it. And nothing will ever change that.

CHAPTER 14

When I step outside, Dad glances over and waves. He points to the phone to indicate that he's still on a call, as if I couldn't see for myself.

I sit on the steps in front of the building. There's nothing to do but listen to Dad talk to work people. The whole time, he says stuff like *As per our earlier conversation, Jim,* and *Let's circle back around to that later, Bob.* I know Dad wants me to grow up and work in an office job like he does, but the last thing I ever want is to have this type of conversation. If I ever go to a job interview and it's with a guy named Jim or Bob, I'm just going to turn around immediately and walk out without a word.

"Okay," he says into the phone. "Sounds good. 'Bye."

He disconnects the call before turning to me. "Sorry about that."

I'm used to it by now. With Dad, work comes first.

"Thought we'd grab a quick bite at Luna with Kate," Dad continues. "She and I have childbirth class later tonight."

I grimace. I don't really like to think about baby stuff, especially birth stuff.

Dad catches my expression. "Don't worry, we'll drop you off at your mom's first."

"Whew!" I say loudly, and we both crack up.

Dad isn't all bad. If we manage to avoid sports and the father-son chats, we're pretty okay. The problem happens when he's in Advice-Dad mode. It feels like he's been stuck there—like *we've* been stuck there—for the past few months. Maybe it's my fault, because of The Incident. Or maybe he's trying to squeeze in all the father-son stuff he can before the new baby comes. The thought makes the happy moment vanish. When I look at Dad, he's watching me carefully.

"Lots of changes are happening," he says. "Is there anything you want to talk about?"

I shrug. I know he's trying to be nice, but some questions feel too big to answer. I think about Dr. Gilmore's ocean painting. Maybe I should carry a picture of a kitchen to help me feel calm.

We turn onto the block where Luna is located, and my mouth starts watering immediately. They say their food is inspired by the American South *and* South America. Their menu includes empanadas, rotisserie meats, and grain bowls. They also make this thing called patacon pisao, which is my favorite. Their version has meat, cheese, slaw, and spicy mayo[21] sandwiched between two plantain disks.

Inside, Kate is already studying the big chalkboard menu. Even though it's a warm spring evening, she's wearing a long cardigan and a pink scarf. She beams when she sees us.

"I haven't been here before," she says. "But it smells so good."

Sometimes I forget that Kate isn't very adventurous with new food. Her idea of *daring* is adding a pinch of freshly ground pepper to a bowl of macaroni and cheese.

"You might like the fish," I tell her. "It comes with jicama pickles." Kate is crazy about pickles.

Her eyes widen. "Oooh, that sounds good. Is it spicy?"

"The sauce has a little heat, but it comes on the side," I tell her.

She turns to Dad. "What are you getting?"

"I had a late lunch—maybe just a salad," he says.

"Their dressing has cilantro in it," I say automatically. "You should see if they could sub oil and vinegar."

Dad gets a funny expression that I can't quite read. He's probably thinking about how much he hates cilantro.

"Thanks, El," he says.

We order at the register and then squeeze into a booth.

---

[21] There is little that makes me more excited than spicy mayo on a sandwich. It is the perfect ingredient.

It's early so it isn't super crowded, but already the line is lengthening. A second chalkboard sign hangs on the wall, listing the farmers they work with. Avery Local—it's everywhere.

"How's your week been so far?" Kate asks.

"Okay," I say.

Dad and Kate exchange glances, and I know in an instant that she must have told him about me crying. Well, if they think I'm going to open up about it right here at dinner, they're wrong. The Tear Tank is officially closed for business.

"We got information about our Avery Local business project," I blurt out.

Dad's face brightens. He loves anything having to do with business. He and Kate ask lots of questions, and I explain about the project.

"You should come to Avery Local," I say. "Both of you."

Kate grins when I say it, and I feel a little pang. I should probably try to include her more, if she's going to be this happy about going to a sixth-grade business fair.

Dad pulls out his phone and taps until his calendar appears. "Tell me what weekend it is. Things have been so busy, and I don't want to miss it."

Wow. Dad's actually using his phone for good! For once, he's listening and cares about something that's important to me. But when I tell him the date, he frowns.

"That weekend I'll be out of town," he says. "I don't know if I'll be back in time."

I try to keep my voice even. "This is important. Can't you reschedule?"

Dad shakes his head. "It's a conference, so it's not like I can change the dates. Besides, we'll be getting close to the baby's due date by then. I won't be traveling after that weekend."

My stomach thuds. Even though the baby isn't here, it seems like he already comes first.

Kate leans forward, ponytail swinging. "I'll still go even if your dad can't make it—and I promise to take lots of pictures."

Dad smiles like it's settled and turns back to his food. Kate is okay, but it's not the same as having Dad there. I shouldn't have acted like I wanted them both to come.

Before long, our food arrives and I dig in.

I watch as Kate takes a bite of her fish. She rolls her eyes in happiness and gives me a big grin. "Agh—this is so good! Thank you for the recommendation."

I can't help but smile back. I like it when I can match up the right food with the right person.

"Tell us more about your project," she says. "Who are you working with?"

"Maribel Martinez," I say. "She's basically a genius and a superstar."

"Well, she sounds like an amazing partner," Kate says.

I nod. "Honestly, I have no idea why she's working with me."

For a moment, I think I might explain what happened with my lunch friends cutting me out—that's a situation where I could maybe use a few words from Advice-Dad. But then Dad looks up.

"I don't like hearing you talk that way, Elliott. You are capable of so much more than you think."

Dad doesn't usually say stuff like that. It feels really good. I chew slowly, stretching out the moment.

"Thanks," I finally manage to say.

He points his fork at me. "It's all a matter of applying yourself. You don't make enough of an effort. If you did, you could be at the top of your class."

I sink low in my seat. Advice-Dad is back, and he's telling me what to do again. Dad's ideas take up so much space that sometimes it feels like there isn't any room left for mine.

Dad pauses to take a breath, and Kate pushes her plate over to him.

"You have to try this—it's so good," she says.

Dad pauses to take a bite. Kate gives me a quick smile. It's almost like she interrupted on purpose. Maybe she didn't want to hear another Dad lecture either.

"What are you doing for the project?" she asks.

"I'm not sure yet," I say.

Dad's forehead wrinkles. "I thought you said the proposal was due soon. Maybe you could do something having to do with science or technology."

That's Dad. Always trying to push me toward subjects I have no interest in.

"We'll talk about it at our next Advisory period," I say. "But I doubt it will have to do with science. Maybe it will have to do with cooking."

The words are out before I had fully thought about them, but it's actually a really good idea. I start to think of the different cooking ideas we could do. Maybe we could make a bunch of spice mixtures for people to cook things with. Or maybe we could even sell food for people to take with them—something they could eat right then or take home for dinner that night.

Kate grins. "Cooking—of course! That's perfect."

Dad's face tightens. I don't know why he's against my project, but I wish he would stop looking at me like that.

"Don't worry, Dad. Whatever it is, it's going to make a lot of money," I blurt out. "So I'm going to be able to pay you back. And then I can go to my camp."

Dad's expression is hard to read. Kate glances at him, then at me, then back to him again.

"That sounds wonderful," she says quietly. "It's good to have a project you're excited about."

I'm not sure that *excited* is the right word, but I don't correct her.

Eventually, Dad nods—just once. "If you can make the money up, you can still go to your camp."

We're all quiet for a moment. Then Kate changes the

subject, launching into a story about something funny that happened on a conference call earlier today.

I can tell by Dad's face that he doesn't think a cooking project is *wonderful*. But he'll change his mind once he sees that I'm able to pay him back. Then he'll have to admit that cooking is something important. Something worthwhile.

CHAPTER 15

The week goes by and suddenly it's Friday morning.

Ms. Choi takes attendance quickly. "Feel free to move around the room to find a spot to work with your group— you can also use the coworking spaces in the hallway. I'm here if you have questions."

Maribel is already heading this way. She plunks her huge binder and pencil case on the desk next to me, then sits down. Today her hair is in a sideways braid. She opens her notebook to a page where *Avery Local* is already written in her curling script. It is a little intimidating, if you want to know the truth.

"Wow," I say. "You're really prepared."

"I'm serious about school projects, you know," Maribel says.

"Me too," I say. "About this one anyway." I explain to her about wanting to make money for culinary camp.

When I finish she nods crisply. "If we work hard, I think we can do it. The Avery Local festival brings in a lot of people."

As she's speaking, a wave of laughter comes from the girls clustered around Parker's desk. Maribel's face tightens.

"Why aren't you working with them?"

She shrugs, not looking up from her paper. "Let's just say I didn't like their project."

Her voice is firm, but it sounds like there's something softer underneath. It sounds like I do when I'm pretending everything is okay.

Behind us, I can hear Gilbert's voice. He and Drew are having one of their *Kingdom of Krull* arguments. This time it's about who's stronger—Wayward Beast or the Glimmering Ogre. For the hundredth time, I think about their catapult project and how fun it sounds. I still can't believe they left me out.

This is one of the worst things about ADHD. Most people know that it stands for attention deficit hyperactivity disorder, but if I'm being honest the name is not all that accurate. *Deficit* means not having enough of something. So if you have a deficit of apples, you don't have enough apples.

This has never been my problem. I have *lots* of apples. Sometimes I have *too many* apples. Sometimes I have so many apples it's like they're spilling out of my arms and rolling across the floor in order to check out a new and exciting fruit basket that's halfway across the room.

It isn't that I *can't* pay attention. It's that I can't always choose which things to pay attention to. For example, sometimes it's easier to pay attention to all the conversations in the room except for the one I'm actually supposed to be participating in. It's definitely harder when I'm in a loud room like this.

Maribel jabs me with her pink gel pen.

I look at her, blinking. "What?"

She tilts her head sideways. "Did you hear anything I just said?"

My cheeks get warm. "Um. No?"

Maribel's face is a mixture of curiosity and frustration. "I was asking what you wanted to do for our project. What are you into? Like . . . sports?"

I frown. "Not all boys are into sports, you know."

Maribel frowns right back. The curiosity from before is gone. This is pure irritation.

"I didn't say it because you're a *boy*," she snaps. "I happen to play volleyball. A girl who actually likes playing sports, can you imagine that?"

Maribel pulls her braid over her shoulder and straightens it. I didn't really know that someone could fix their hair in an angry way, but that's what she's doing all right. I gulp. I really messed this up, and I'm not even sure how it happened.

"Sorry," I say. "How about something cooking related?"

Her face brightens. "Cooking! I can work with that."

She leans over the page and starts writing. From time to time she looks up and says something, and I just nod or say *yes*. The page slowly fills with pink ink.

Before long, I am completely lost.

I want to pay attention to this conversation, I really do. Maribel is working hard. And she's actually trying to keep me involved in the process—probably a lot more than Victor and Gilbert would have done. But the truth is—even though it's barely nine o'clock—for me, it feels like it's already been a very long day. The conversations in this room are so loud, it's hard not to pay attention to what everyone else is doing. My brain feels like a giant tangle of yarn, and I can't find the right thread to follow.

But I can't let Maribel know I'm not paying attention. So even though I'm not sure what we're talking about anymore, I keep smiling and nodding.

I may not know what our project is going to be about, but at least I gave her the idea for cooking. I may not be good at much, but I'm probably the best chef in our grade. So I know everything will be okay.

It has to be.

CHAPTER 16

I open the front door and drop my backpack on the floor. "I'm home!"

There's no answer, even though I saw Mom's car in the driveway. Then I hear her—she's probably on a work call in her office. She got a big promotion last summer, and now she takes more calls from home—not as many as Dad though.

I check Denver and Omelet's food and water as I say hello to them—I know Mom will take care of them when I'm at Dad's, but I like to make sure everything is topped off.

Every Friday afternoon is the same—Dad swings by on his way from work to pick me up for my weekend visit.

That's why I'm surprised to see Kate's silver SUV pull

up in front of our house. She doesn't pull into the driveway, like Dad, but parks out front. After a moment, the door opens and she does a kind of half step/half jump out of the car. I can't say for sure, but sometimes it seems like being pregnant is kind of awkward.

Kate stands by the car, like she doesn't know if she should come knock or what. I push open the screen door and stick my head out.

"Hey," I say. "Hi."

She turns and looks at me and does a little wave. She's wearing a sweater that seems to crisscross and have lots of layers. Kate likes complicated clothing.

"Hi! Your dad has a late meeting tonight, so he asked me to come get you," she says. "I hope that's okay."

I hesitate just for a moment. "Yeah. Of course."

Her face looks uncertain, and I guess mine probably does too. Dad's always the one who picks me up, every Friday like clockwork ever since The Divorce.

"I just need to grab my stuff," I say. "Do you want to come in? Or . . ."

"Oh!" Kate smooths her sweater over her belly. "No. That's okay. I can wait."

And then Mom is behind me. "Out or in, Elliott, don't leave the door wide open—oh, Kate! Hello!"

Kate pats her hair, which doesn't have a strand out of place. "Hi, Nina—I'm so sorry, I should have texted. I'm picking up Elliott because Mark got tied up at work."

"Elliott, go on and get your things," Mom says. Then she turns to Kate. "How are you feeling these days?"

I go down the hallway and get my bag. I say a silent thank-you to Thursday Elliott, who remembered to do laundry. He didn't remember to put things away, but at least it's clean. I run to the dryer and pick out socks, shorts, shirts, and underwear to cover me for the weekend.

When I go back outside, Kate is thanking Mom for the baby gift. I want to jam my fingers in my ears so I don't hear a word but can't think of a way to do it casually.

"So kind of you—" Kate coos.

"I couldn't resist!" Mom answers.

"It really meant a lot to me," Kate says back.

"It was just a little thing," Mom replies. "No trouble at all."

It is an epic battle of overpoliteness that shows no sign of ending. We could be here for hours[22] if I don't do something to stop them.

I strategically position myself within arm's reach of Mom and hold up my backpack to show her.

"I got everything. 'Bye, Mom," I say.

As expected, I get a giant hug in return.

"Have a good time, honey! Love you!"

I follow Kate to her car. I climb in beside her and do my seat belt. It's just as neat and tidy as Dad's, with that same

[22] Possibly days.

scent of lemon-fresh wipes. Someone should tell companies that this is nowhere close to the smell of a real lemon, which is around a thousand times better. Or maybe that's why they call it *lemon fresh* and not just *lemon*. They know there's no way to compare to the real thing.

Then I realize that Kate is saying something.

"—busy at work, I know he wanted to pick you up."

We're driving by the purple house. There's a dad pushing a kid on a tire swing. I look the other way.

"That's all right," I say.

We drive past the rocket slide, which has a bunch of little kids playing on it, and then go through their neighborhood streets. Kate pulls into the garage, and I jump out and go inside. Then I run upstairs to put away my backpack—I know from experience Dad's fury when I leave my things on the floor.

When I come back downstairs, Kate is in the kitchen. In the car, she seemed happy and energetic, but now she looks tired. She stares out the window, touching the sides of her head lightly.

I hesitate, not sure what to do. But then she turns and sees me.

"Any ideas for dinner? We could order pizza if you want," she says, back to her regular, bubbly self.

I open the fridge to see what's there—Kate's peach-flavored water, a couple of takeout containers, three jars of pickles, a bunch of purple grapes, a couple of wedges of cheese, two limes, and a big . . . round . . . *cabbage?* One of these things is not like the others.

"What's the deal with this?" I ask, holding it up.

Kate blushes. "Oh—nothing. It's kind of funny, I guess. I got it because—well, because our book says that's the size the baby is now."

I heft the cabbage in my hand. I'm the first to admit that I know nothing about babies, but that seems pretty big to me. "Really? That's interesting."

She looks at me warily. To be fair, I have a history of not taking news about the baby very well. See also: The Incident.

"Do you want to see the book?" she asks, like she's thinking (hoping?) I'll say no.

"Okay," I say. "I mean—sure."

She plucks a volume from the shelf. It's a soothing green on the outside and says *Week by Week: Grown with Love.* She flips open to week 30 and shows me the illustration of a cabbage.

"Next week is a bunch of leeks," she says

I move toward her for a closer look. "That definitely seems like cheating. How many leeks and what size? That's not as good of a visual as a cabbage. Plus, they're different shapes."

Kate laughs. "I completely agree."

She turns pages through the different weeks. I glimpse a napa cabbage, a pineapple, a cantaloupe, romaine lettuce, and a pumpkin.

I'm about to object again—are they talking about size or weight? Because obviously a cantaloupe is heavier than lettuce.

"This guide feels like someone wandered around in a grocery store, randomly assigning produce to each week," I say.

Kate nods. "Wait until you see this."

She turns the page again, and taps Week 40—the final week—and the picture is a watermelon. A *watermelon*.

My eyes widen. "*Seriously?* Is this book trying to scare people or what?"

Kate nods vigorously. "That's what I said too!"

"I mean . . . *ouch!*" I start lumbering around the kitchen, holding out my arms like I have a giant watermelon baby inside me.

Kate snickers and starts walking around the same way, her feet thudding on the floor—which is very un-Kate of her. But now we're both cracking up, and for some reason it's even funnier because she really *does* have a cabbage-sized baby inside her, which will someday be watermelon-sized, which is both ridiculous and unreasonable—and probably pretty uncomfortable too.

So that's why we don't even hear when Dad walks in and is standing in the kitchen holding a pizza.

He looks at us like we've both lost our minds. "What's going on?"

I grin. "Not much. Just learning about cabbages and watermelon."

Kate giggles.

Dad looks back and forth between us. He's shaking his head slowly, but he's smiling. "Well. I brought mushroom-and-onion."

"Oh, Dad," I say. "The baby was an onion *weeks* ago."

Kate cracks up, and then I laugh even harder, and soon Dad is laughing too. We all grab a slice and eat right there, standing up in the kitchen, and honestly? It actually feels okay.

PART THREE

School-Project Pie

PINEAPPLE, CHERRIES, PECANS, MARASCHINO CHERRY JUICE, CORNFLAKES, RAISINS

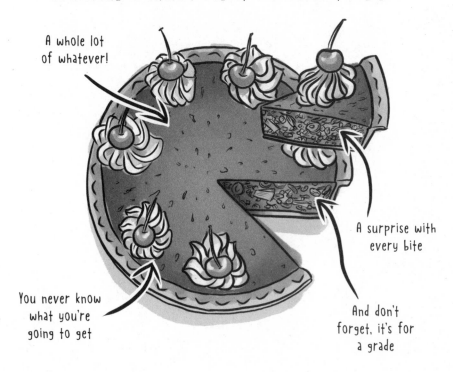

A whole lot of whatever!

A surprise with every bite

You never know what you're going to get

And don't forget, it's for a grade

CHAPTER 17

Seeing as the project proposal is due today, I'm guessing that Maribel and I will spend most of the Advisory period talking about it.

"Okay, everyone," Ms. Choi says. "Listen up! No announcements today—please use the entire class for project time. You don't have to stay inside the classroom—feel free to spread out into the hall."

That's the best idea I've heard all week. I know I'll have a better chance of staying focused if I can convince Maribel to move away from the busy classroom.

"Can we go somewhere quieter?" I ask.

She nods, grabbing a pink three-ring binder and her pencil pouch.

We find a coworking space that's over by the window. I take the seat that backs up to the glass.[23]

Maribel sits on a boxy chair, pulling her legs beneath her. She holds up the binder. "Here's the proposal."

She opens the notebook and starts flipping pages. There are color-coded tabs. There are labeled charts. There are spreadsheets on top of spreadsheets. And there's one word I keep seeing over and over again. Pie. Pie. Pie. Pie. Not pie charts. But . . . pie. Actual pie.

My eyes go round. "What's this?"

Maribel looks at me sideways. "This is our project," she says slowly.

"But you've done it already!" I say.

"The proposal is due today," she says. "Did you think I was going to leave it until the last minute?"

I shake my head slowly. "But there are so many pages. This is just the proposal?"

Maribel shrugs. "It's the stuff we talked about—I typed it, that's all."

I grab the binder, shaking it. "Spreadsheets! We did not discuss spreadsheets!"

At least, I think we didn't.

Maribel's cheeks redden. "I happen to love spreadsheets. What's wrong with that?"

As I turn the pages, I start to feel dizzy. I try taking deep

---

[23] Windows were basically invented for distraction purposes.

breaths, but it's as if my lungs were replaced with tiny bal-
loons that refuse to inflate.

I stab the page with my finger. "But . . . *pie*?"

Maribel snatches the binder from my hands. "We definitely discussed pies on Friday. You said you liked cooking,
and I said I like pie. Why are you acting like this?"

I wince, remembering. Friday Elliott did nod and agree
his way through a conversation that he wasn't paying attention to. But that doesn't mean Monday Elliott is happy
about it.

"I said I liked *cooking*," I said. "Not *baking*."

Griffin Connor's face pops into my head. *Baking is not real
cooking. No one's palate was ever elevated by a sugar-bomb.*

Maribel's eyebrows turn into straight-across lines. "Well,
I happen to like *baking*. Besides, a few days ago you said it
was okay! Did you change your mind or something?"

I gulp. "Um. So. When we talked, I may not have been
fully paying attention."

Maribel's eyes widen. "What does that mean?"

I look down. "I have ADHD. Sometimes I have a hard
time focusing."

My voice sounds awkward and clumsy. I'm not used to
talking about my ADHD with anyone but my parents or
Dr. Gilmore or Malcolm, before he moved away.

"I'm sorry," I say.

When I look up again, Maribel's face is softer. Not a lot,
but a little.

"It's okay," she says. "I guess."

"Can I see the binder again?" I ask.

Silently, she pushes it across the table again.

I turn the pages, trying hard to keep an open mind. Did Maribel really say she loves spreadsheets? I may not be a numbers person, but I can tell that she worked hard on this. I read the pages one by one. Her plan is that we make pies and sell them at the festival. Okay. I've never made a pie, but I've eaten plenty of them in my life. Maybe I can work with this idea.

Then I see two words that make me feel like the walls are closing in.

"Um," I say. "Why are the pies gluten-free?"

Maribel's frown gets deeper. "Because they're going to be."

Inwardly, I groan. Griffin Connor also has a lot to say about the trend of people eating gluten-free. None of it is nice.

Maybe Maribel needs me to explain it to her.

"Gluten is *good*. It's what makes dough stretchy," I say.

"I know that," Maribel snaps. Her voice is crisp.

I don't understand why she's so mad. "Then what's the problem? Are we just going to have weird trendy food? Because I can assure you that no one will want to eat it."

"Some people will," Maribel says.

I scoff. "Like who?"

Maribel frowns. "People with celiac disease."

I roll my eyes. "Yes, but—"

Maribel scowls. "People like me."

Oh.[24]

Maribel waves her hands as she speaks. "I am tired of people acting like I eat this way because of a fad. Don't you think I would rather eat regular foods? Trust me, I would if I could."

"Maribel, listen—" I say.

She ignores me. "And not only that, people act like gluten-free is a *joke*. It's like shorthand for saying someone is picky or annoying. Well, it's not my fault that my stomach can't handle it. It's not my fault that every time I have a speck of it, I throw up for hours. Or worse."

I gulp. "Or worse?"

"Trust me," she says ominously. "You do *not* want to know."

I straighten my glasses. "I'm sorry, Maribel. I didn't know it was a real thing."

Maribel nods. "You should know, since you say you want to be a chef and everything. But a *lot* of people think it's fake. Even some of my supposed friends."

My eyebrows go up. I'm not an expert on friendship, but I know that Malcolm never acted like he didn't believe me about my ADHD.

---

[24] I wish I could take my words back. I'd chop, sauté, and eat them, if I only could.

She leans across the table and talks in a whisper. "Maybe not all of them. But ever since I got diagnosed, it is like Kennedy is against me. She even brought a backpack stuffed full of gluten snacks to a sleepover at my house. It really makes me mad."

"Is that why you aren't working with them?" I ask.

Maribel looks down for a moment, then looks up again. She's fiddling with her side braid. I start to think that I shouldn't have asked—that I went too far. But then she clears her throat.

"I was *going* to work with them," she says finally. "We were going to do cupcakes. But then on Monday Kennedy said that they couldn't be gluten-free because gluten-free is gross. And everyone said okay because everyone always goes along with Kennedy."

I think about her words. I always thought that having a big group of friends would make things easier. But maybe not.

"Anyway," she continues. "I think they thought I would still work with them, even if I couldn't eat the cupcakes. But flour is easy to breathe in if someone's using a mixer. It's a bad idea for me to be around it."

I nod. "Whenever I use it, it somehow gets everywhere."

Maribel manages a small smile, but then she shakes her head as if to clear it. "When Parker realized I was going to switch groups, she said maybe they should do gluten-free after all."

My eyebrows rise. "So why didn't you?"

Maribel shrugs. "I said it was fine, that I would work with you. Kennedy said *okay* really quick. I didn't feel like I could take it back."

I shake my head. "That's not nice."

She nods. "I didn't really want to work with them anymore—not like that. You know?"

"I do know," I say slowly. I explain how Victor and my lunch friends didn't want me in their group because I'm not focused enough.

I'm afraid she is going to agree with them—after all, I *did* somehow miss the entire conversation about our project topic.

But Maribel just nods. "Sometimes, people can be mean. Especially to people who are different."

I nod, thinking about my lunch friends. I'm not sure what I would do if they invited me to work with them now. But then I think about the group chat and the completely offensive *no offense*. For some things, there are no take backs.

Maribel leans forward. "This is why I'm counting on you, Elliott. We need to show them. I haven't made pie before, but it can't be that hard, can it?"

I open my mouth to say something, but she's still speaking, leaning forward in her seat.

"I don't just need these pies to be gluten-free. I need these pies to be gluten-free and *absolutely delicious*. Because otherwise, Kennedy is going to make fun of them. She'll say they're gross, and everyone will go along with her, just because she's Kennedy."

The binder lies open between us. Maribel's done so much work already. She's thought through the budget, our signs—even the booth design. She is unstoppable, like a laser beam. This project is about more than just a grade for her. For me too.

Maybe this is something I can give in on. Besides, baking is easy. People will be excited about sweets. We'll sell a bunch—maybe enough that I can do what I really want to do. I can make paella with my eyes closed. How hard could it be to make a few pies? I'll be able to pay back Dad and go to camp, which is all that really matters.

"Sure, we can do that," I say. "No problem."

She grins and I grin back. Today Elliott and Today Maribel might not know how to bake pies, but that's a problem for Future Elliott and Future Maribel to handle.

CHAPTER 18

My stomach grumbles, so I head to the kitchen. I'm in the mood for one of my Legendary Snack Bowls™. They're different every time.

The rules are:
1. I can only use leftovers—nothing freshly made.
2. There must be something crunchy on top.
3. I have to eat them with a spoon—no other utensils.

From the fridge, I grab a container of hummus, a dozen baby carrots, two hard-boiled eggs, some of yesterday's tuna salad, and a hearty glob of sunflower butter. This all goes into the same bowl, which I mash and spread around a little.

Then I sprinkle crushed corn chips on top. A little sticky but definitely delicious.

Mom comes into the kitchen and puts her half-empty mug of coffee in the microwave. This is classic Mom—she makes coffee, then gets so busy working she forgets to drink it. When she discovers it's cold, she puts it in the microwave. She basically rewarms the same mug of coffee all day.

She looks across the kitchen at me. "Legendary Snack Bowl?"

I nod.

"Can I try a bite?" She grabs a spoon from the drawer. "Hmm, interesting. I think I like it. How was school today?"

I swallow my bite of food, which takes a while on account of its stickiness. "Maribel wrote an entire project proposal about us baking pie for our business plan."

The microwave beeps, and Mom rescues her coffee from what's probably its tenth rewarming. When she turns to look at me, her eyebrows are raised. "Did you say . . . *baking?*"

"Yeah." On the inside I brace myself for a joke about pies not being *real.*

But Mom just sips her coffee. "I see."

"Is it okay if we use our kitchen to practice in?" I ask.

She grins, setting her mug on the counter. "Yes, as long as you promise that I'll get to sample whatever you make."

I swallow a big bite. "Sure."

She plants a kiss on top of my head.

Secretly, I don't mind, but I pull away anyhow. "*Mom*."

She throws her hands in the air. "I know, I know! You're too big for random smooches. But, come on! It's just— Elliott, baking! I can't wait to see what you make."

Before I can answer, she picks up her coffee mug and shuffles down the hall to her desk. As she walks away, I can still hear her muttering, "Who would have ever thought?"

I smile to myself. Maybe she's surprised about me baking. But I'm surprised too—about lots of things. About a baking project. About a new friend coming over. About the perfect grade I'm going to get on this school project. And the fact that I'm going to pay Dad back—and maybe have some left over.

Who would have ever thought? Definitely not me.

CHAPTER 19

Saturday afternoon, while Kate was at pregnancy yoga, Dad and I watched the newest *Clone of the Stars* movie, part 17. Then it was time to meet Kate for dinner at Arcelia's.

We get to the restaurant first and Dad lets me order some appetizers. I scoop a ridiculous amount of guacamole[25] on my tortilla chip and cram it into my mouth. "Did you like the movie, Dad? I thought it was the best so far."

Dad's phone buzzes, and he pulls it from his pocket. He starts typing on it.

I spear a chunk of carrot and look around the room. I've been coming here my whole life—its brick walls and striped vinyl booths are imprinted in my memory.

---

[25] Is there ever such a thing as too much guacamole? I don't think so.

Dad doesn't look up from his phone. "Mmm," he says distractedly.

I take a big drink of water. All the popcorn followed by chips is making me thirsty.

"Hi, guys," Kate says, sliding into the booth on Dad's side. She's wearing a fluffy white sweater over her workout clothes.

"Hi, Kate," I say.

Dad pockets his phone, and she gives him a quick kiss. I pretend to be very interested in the wall.

Kate picks the cauliflower and carrots out of the escabeche, carefully avoiding the jalapeños.

The server, a tall guy with his hair in a ponytail, comes by to take our orders. Dad wants enchiladas. Kate asks for chicken tacos. I get albondigas soup. It's my personal goal to eat every item on the menu, which happens to be eight pages long. I'm currently working my way through the soups-and-stews section.

"So," Kate says, turning to me. "What have you been up to?"

"We watched *Clone of the Stars* this afternoon," I say.

"How was it?" Kate asks.

Dad shrugs, making a *meh* gesture with his hands.

It feels like a betrayal. "Dad! You said you liked it."

Dad shakes his head. "Not anywhere close to the best. The early ones were so much stronger. This is like a watered-down version."

I arch an eyebrow. "So you liked it better when you could see the strings holding the glow whales as they float through space? Okay, I'll keep that in mind."

Dad chuckles. "The effects are fantastic, I'll give you that. But the story? The characters? It's just not the same as it was before. I miss the old days."

"I totally disagree," I say. "Besides, the old movies are super weird. Why don't the women get better roles? And what about the aliens, like—why are the humans automatically superior to them?"

"If the aliens want better roles, they should make movies themselves," Dad says jokingly.

I push my plate around my side of the table. If Dad didn't like the movie, I wish he'd said something before—not waited to say it until after Kate was here.

"Stop fidgeting," Dad says.

"I'm *not*," I answer, even though I am. I can't help it.

The server comes by and brings me another Coke—filled to the very top and with a decent amount of ice, which I appreciate. Arcelia's has good ice in tiny cubes—perfect for chomping.

"Don't bite ice," Dad says. "That will ruin your tooth enamel."

He acts like he knows everything, but he doesn't. I'm not a baby, but he treats me like one anyway. He'll even stop me from going to camp, which I've been looking forward to all year.

"No, it won't," I say. I keep crunching.

Dad gives me a look.

I slide more ice into my mouth and chew it while Dad watches. I'm being stubborn. But I'm mad about him suddenly trashing *Clone of the Stars* in front of Kate.

Dad frowns. "It's unpleasant. Let's just enjoy our meal."

"Fine." I set down my glass a little harder than I mean to. The ice inside jostles.

"Careful," Dad says.

"I *am* careful," I say.

I grab a handful of chips and crunch those instead. Dad shrugs, glancing at Kate with a *"Kids!"* kind of look, which makes me even more mad.

Kate squeezes his hand. "Did you want to . . . ?"

Dad looks over at me. "We wanted to talk to you about the baby's middle name."

Kate grins. "We're thinking of a special name—a family name."

Faster than a glow whale jumping into hyperspeed, I know exactly what they're going to say. *A family name.* They're going to give the new baby *Quigley* for a middle name—the same middle name that Dad and I have.

It's not fair. I'm already sharing Dad with the new baby. I'm already sharing that house—where he'll live all the time while I'm just a weekend visitor. I don't want to have to share *Quigley* with him too.

I try to take a deep breath, but I forget my mouth is full of food. A tortilla chip wedges in my throat, and I start coughing wildly. Shards of chips spray everywhere.[26]

Kate's eyes widen. "Do you need water?"

I reach for my glass, but I'm coughing so hard my aim isn't

---

[26] If I weren't so busy being mortified, I'd be pretty grossed out right now.

129

very good. My hand hits the side, and as I'm pulling back to try to fix it, I stick my hand in the guacamole with a squish. I pull it out as fast as I can but bump into my Coke. By the time I'm done, my hand is covered in avocado and both of my glasses have spilled their contents across the table, the paper placemats, the bowl of chips, and onto Kate and Dad.

"Oh!" Kate says, patting at the brown stain spreading on her sweater.

Dad's face turns the same red as the salsa. "Elliott, what's gotten into you? I told you to be careful!"

Everyone in the restaurant is staring at me. I'm a mess. I'm also *mortified*.

Tears spring into my eyes. I wipe at them, but it's no use. The tears run down my cheeks.

Oh no. The sports-announcer Tear Tank is back.

Introducing Elliott! On the outside he may look like a regular, everyday kid—one with very messy hair, but still a regular kid—but he's actually a modern marvel. Consisting of 99.9 percent water, this kid threatens to overflow at any time. Behold the Human Crying Machine!

I keep crying, wiping at the table.

"It's okay," Kate says. "Accidents happen to everyone."

Maybe it's the kind of thing that could happen to anyone, but mostly it feels like the kind of thing that's always happening to *me*.

CHAPTER 20

Somehow, I manage to make it through the rest of the meal without knocking over anything else.

When we're done, we all go outside.

"What now?" Dad asks.

"I think I'll check out the tea shop over on Market," Kate says. "Why don't you and Elliott have some time together? I'll meet you at home."

Kate kisses Dad goodbye and heads down the street, her yoga bag slung over her shoulder.

Dad and I look at each other. "Ice cream?" he asks.

"I'm not really hungry," I say.

"Okay," Dad says. "Let's walk around a bit."

We head south, walking through a knot of people clustered outside a bar. There are some statues of crickets outside—for the baseball team, I guess. Some kids are swinging on the antennae.

Dad catches my eye. "Want to go see the City River?"

City River is what my family calls this series of fountains that's interconnected by a series of waterways, tucked away in a brick courtyard that's almost completely surrounded by tall buildings. There are all kinds of places to explore. Paths, stairs, stepping stones, and bridges crisscross the streams. When I was little, I was sure that it was a real river, right in the city. Now I know better, of course, but I guess the name just stuck.

We cross the street and walk between the brick buildings. I can hear the rushing water before I can see it. There's a restaurant with tables in one area, a small grassy lawn with people tossing a Frisbee on the other. Everywhere there are lights strung overhead and the sound of rushing water.

Dad grins. "I haven't been over here for a while. I forgot how much I love this place."

Together, we wander over a bridge and onto the path that looks like stepping stones while we check out the fountains. We stop at one that is designed to look like a waterfall. When I was little, I was afraid of it—I thought maybe I'd get sucked in or something—but right now I feel calm looking at it. It's nice to stand here like this, with Dad, the water roaring all around us. Maybe this is why Dr. Gilmore likes the ocean so much.

I want to say lots of things to Dad. Like how much I miss

doing this stuff with him. How I want to make sure there's time for just us, even after the baby comes.

Like he's reading my mind, Dad pats me on the shoulder.

But then he ruins it.

"Let's talk about what happened at dinner," he says. "I think you could have handled that better."

My face flushes hot. Leave it to Dad to bring up an awkward moment instead of just letting us have a normal time together.

"It's always about what I do wrong! It's never about what I do right."

Dad's face turns red. I can tell he's trying to keep his patience. "Elliott, calm down."

Has anyone in the entire history of the universe ever gotten calmer when someone tells them to *calm down*?[27]

I squeeze my hands and then release them. Squeeze and release, squeeze and release.

Dad is watching me. "Okay? Are you ready to talk?"

I shrug. "Am I in trouble?"

Dad's cheeks puff as he lets out a long breath. "You're not in trouble, Elliott."

There's something I don't understand in his voice—sadness? He rubs his hands in little circles on his temples like I'm giving him a headache.

~~~~~~

[27] Nope.

133

"I'm trying, okay?" he asks. "Can you try to meet me halfway?"

I look at him sideways. This sounds like the kind of thing Mom would say.

He takes a deep breath. "You got so upset at dinner. What was that about?"

The easy answer is that I was upset because I knocked over my soda. But *easy* is not the same as *honest*.

I clear my throat. "I was embarrassed. But then when I cried, I got even more embarrassed. I really hate crying."

Dad looks surprised. "What do you mean? You mean you hate that you cried at a restaurant?"

"I mean crying anywhere," I say glumly.

He frowns. "Crying isn't necessarily a bad thing, Elliott."

"It would be one thing if I did it only when I was sad," I say. "But that's not it—most of the time it just happens when I'm having lots of feelings. It's like they're fighting inside me, trying to get out and they can't. So they make my Tear Tank overflow."

The words come out in a rush. I wince after I realize what I've said. I've never told anyone about the Tear Tank. It's the kind of thing that Dad might make a joke about—a flip comment. Something to make it seem smaller than it is. I brace myself.

Dad's phone chimes—but he doesn't reach for it. For once, he doesn't seem to notice it.

Instead, Dad scratches behind his ear, which is what he

does when he's thinking hard. "I wonder if the problem is that you're feeling so many things at once. Maybe it would help to talk about just *one* of the feelings."

I look at him, open mouthed. This doesn't sound like my dad. And it doesn't sound like a TV-show dad. It's like someone else entirely.

"It's an idea I got from—from someone I've been talking to." There's a note of hesitation that *really* doesn't seem like Dad.

I pause, tilting my head sideways, trying to figure it out.

"You don't have to if you don't want to," he adds quickly.

"I'm just thinking," I say.

Dad looks at me steadily. I know he's waiting, but it isn't easy to start talking out of the blue. To be honest, I don't know if I can trust Dad. He might ruin it at any moment. He might make a joke. He might begin to outline a plan for Elliott-improvement. I don't want that.

"But just one," I say. "And you have to promise you won't give me any advice. And no follow-up questions."

"I promise," he says.

There's so much I want to talk to him about. I want to tell him why camp is so important to me. I want to explain how I feel about The Incident—how I worry that it made Dad so disappointed in me. I also want to tell him how I feel about the baby. When I think of that one, it hurts—like pushing on a bruise that isn't quite healed. It feels like the hardest thing to talk about—but maybe it's also the most important.

"I'm scared," I say. "About the baby."

I can tell Dad is taking it in. Even in the evening light, I can see his expressions change as he thinks about what I said. He doesn't speak for a very long time. But eventually, he nods. "Okay. Thanks for telling me."

And that's it—we keep walking. No advice. It's a small thing. It's not a perfect thing. But it's a good moment for Dad and me. Honestly, it's one of the best we've had in a very long time.

CHAPTER 21

Maribel Martinez is coming over this afternoon so we can make pie.

I never knew this before, but people with celiac disease have to be really careful with what they eat. Even a tiny speck of gluten can make them feel sick for days. So before Maribel came over, our moms talked and made a plan to make sure everything was safe for her. This means squeaky-clean counters, bowls, and utensils. No using any butter that might have bread crumbs in it. Mom even bought a new colander, just to be on the safe side.

The idea of Maribel coming over makes me feel a bit jumpy. I arrange the butter and salt next to the strawberries from the farmers' market. Then I decide I should probably wipe down the counters a fourth time. I would feel terrible if she got sick because of me.

Mom comes in the kitchen when I'm scrubbing the sink.

"What's up, El?" she asks. "Are you nervous about something?"

I shrug. "It's just that no one has really been over since Malcolm left. It feels kind of weird." I don't get into the fact that Maribel is both popular and a genius, which, let's be honest, is a challenging combination.

Mom pats my hand. "It will be fine. Just be yourself."

Easy for her to say.

When the doorbell rings, I almost jump out of my chair. But when I open the door, I don't see Popular Maribel or Genius Maribel. I see regular old Maribel, a three-ring binder in one hand and a grocery bag in the other.

She grins. "Our secret ingredient—gluten-free flour."

I take the package from her and tell her thanks. I was glad when she offered to buy the flour—I wouldn't have known which one to pick.

Our first stop is Denver and Omelet's cage. Her eyes light up when she sees them. "They're so cute! Remind me which one is which."

I show her, and she pets them both. "You have the most fabulous hair," she says, patting Denver. "And you have the sweetest face," she says to Omelet. He cuddles against her hand like he's ready to pack his suitcases and move to her house.

Mom sticks her head in the room. "Hi, Maribel. I'm Elliott's mom, Nina."

Maribel looks up from the guinea pigs. "I love all the things on your walls."

I can tell Mom is happy that Maribel likes our house, and I am too. Our house has a lot of personal things in it, so if someone likes them, then it feels as though they like us too.

"Maribel, will you need a ride home afterward? I'm happy to drop you off so your parents don't have to double back," Mom says.

Maribel shakes her head. "They're shopping downtown and said they'll pick me up after."

Mom smiles at both of us. "I'll be in the office catching up on some paperwork. Holler if you need me."

Mom heads down the hall to her room. Maribel and I are quiet for a moment. She's rubbing behind Omelet's ears, and he has a look of total bliss on his face.

"Ready to get started?" I ask her.

Maribel nods and follows me to the kitchen.

"Whoa," she says. "Someone really likes plants."

"Yeah—my mom," I answer. Maribel looks at all the plants, including the avocado pit in its jar. It's just as unimpressive as ever.

I show her where we can wash our hands. Maribel goes first.

"I was thinking that I can make the crust while you make the filling," I say. "Unless you want to do it the other way?"

She dries her hands on a kitchen towel. "That's fine. Did you print out a recipe?"

I shake my head. "I don't use recipes." Does my voice sound snide? Maybe a little. I prefer to think of it as Griffin-Connoresque.

"Okaaay," she says slowly, stretching out the word. "Why not?"

"Griffin Connor says that recipes aren't *real* cooking. A real chef needs ingredients and techniques only."

I nod in the direction of the counter, where I've already set out ingredients. I've even remembered to put out equipment we might need, including mixing bowls, spoons, and a glass pie pan. It's good that Maribel gets to see me in this environment, where I'm so detail oriented.

Maribel looks at me skeptically. "What's the plan, then— mixing stuff together? That doesn't seem like much of a technique."

My ears feel warm. "It's a pie, not rocket science. Only a Muffinhead would think pie making is difficult." I try to make my voice sound confident, like Griffin Connor's.

Maribel rolls her eyes, which is annoying. Oh well. It's not my fault she lacks confidence.

I claim the big stainless steel bowl and add some flour and a pinch of salt. Then I stir in some water. Then I add some more.

"How does it look?" I ask.

Maribel peers at the bowl. "It looks . . . wet. *Too* wet."

I study the crust mixture. She has a point. "No problem. If it's wet, it needs more dry stuff. I'll add more flour."

"Are you *sure* we don't need a recipe?" Maribel asks.

Anger flashes inside me. I'm tired of people not taking me seriously.

"I told you—recipes are for losers!" In the small kitchen, my voice echoes a bit. That came out a little stronger than I meant it to be.

Maribel takes a step backward. "Yikes. Calm down."

I close my eyes and take a breath. "Sorry, I just meant to say that we can figure out the right proportions by eyeballing it."

She narrows her eyes. "So, you're saying that only a Muffinhead would follow a recipe—"

I smile, glad she finally understands. "Exactly."

"—But instead, we should *follow* whatever Griffin Connor says to do," she continues. "Is that right?"

It feels like a trick question.

"Um," I say. "Yes. No. Sort of."

Maribel rolls her eyes. "Whatever. You make the crust. I'll do the filling. Using a *recipe*."

Before I can say a word, she pulls out her phone and starts searching.

This isn't how I imagined today going. We are partners—we should work together.

"Wait a minute—" I start to say.

But Maribel is shaking her head. "You do your thing, and I'll do mine."

After a few moments, she seems to find what she's looking for. She stares at the screen, reading carefully. Then she puts the berries in the colander and rinses them.

I scowl, turning back to my bowl. Maybe she's going to use a recipe, but it doesn't mean I have to. And I bet mine will turn out better.

Even though I've never made a crust, I've seen Griffin Connor make savory pies. It seems straightforward. The ingredients are flour, butter, and water. The butter makes little pockets of air form in the crust so it will be flaky and tender. The water helps the flour stick together.

I glance over at Maribel. She's already finished washing the strawberries and cutting off their green tops. "How's your filling going?"

"Spectacular," she says evenly. Even without seeing her face, I can tell she's still annoyed. Before today, I never knew shoulders could look angry.

"Just so you know," I say. "My piecrust over here is amazing."

She doesn't answer, just scoops the small heap of green leaves into the bin.

In the bowl, my dough is looking a little soupy. Probably the butter will help. Butter always makes things better. I add some more in and then start mixing.

The good news is that it seems to be clumping together.

The bad news is that it's too thick to stir.

I just need a stronger spoon, that's all. When I go to grab it, I notice that Maribel has made a neat pile of berries, cut to the same thickness. That may sound easy, but it's actually tricky—especially on something that's strawberry shaped.

"Hey," I say. "Nice knife skills."

Maribel keeps slicing. "Thanks."

Back at my spot at the counter, I manage to stir the whole mess into a roundish mass. Tilting the bowl, I prod the dough ball until it rolls onto the counter with a thud.

Maribel measures cornstarch and sugar, precisely leveling each scoop before adding them. She heats the mixture over a saucepan, and the smell of strawberries fills the room.

She glances at me. "This recipe calls for vanilla. Do you have any?"

I get the bottle from the pantry and watch as she reads the label.

"I have to be super careful," she says. "Once I even found *salt* that had been processed with gluten."

"Oh." I don't really know what to say. I can't imagine what it would be like to have to be on alert all the time.

I look at my pile of crust. It doesn't look quite right, but I don't know how to fix it. Griffin Connor made it seem like it was easy—that all I needed was flour, butter, and water. But it seems like something's missing.

Maybe what it's missing is strength. I attack the crust with the marble rolling pin, mashing as hard as I can.

"Wow," I say. "This crust is coming along great. Super easy. Didn't even need a recipe."

Maribel raises her eyebrows. "My berries are *also* great. And they're almost done."

Already? I start rolling faster, but as the dough flattens, it begins to stick to the counter. I sprinkle another handful of flour on top.

Maribel holds her phone next to the filling. "Perfect—it matches the photo exactly."

"Let me guess," I say. "Is it one of those ridiculous cooking blogs with a zillion photos? Like, picture one: this is a stick of butter. Picture two: this is an *unwrapped* stick of butter. Picture three: a *melted* stick of butter. Who needs pictures of every little step?"

Maribel whirls in my direction. "Who cares what other people do? Not everyone needs Griffin Connor's approval on every little thing."

"Well, they should," I say. "Because Griffin Connor is an absolute genius."

"Absolute genius? More like an absolute *snob*," Maribel says.

I glare at her. "He is not! Griffin Connor says that recipes disrupt the creative process," I say hotly. "Besides, they're not any fun."

Maribel shakes her head. "Oh, right—because you're having so much *fun* murdering that piecrust. Honestly, Elliott, what did that poor crust ever do to you?"

She shoves the bowl of pie filling across the counter. We stare at each other.

I wish we could go back to when she first arrived. When we were playing with the guinea pigs it seemed like we were friends. Everything was fine before we started working in the kitchen. Now it seems like we're on opposite sides.

"Listen," I start to say.

But then Maribel's phone chimes. She looks at the screen and starts texting, basically ignoring me. That's okay. I don't need her anyway.

I turn back to the crust. It's not rolling out in a thin circle like it should. Instead, it's lumpy and kind of grayish. I scrape it off the counter and try to flatten it into the pie pan. The dough doesn't lie neatly like it's supposed to. There's a big gash along one side. This is so much harder than it looked on Griffin Connor's demonstration.

I patch the ripped area with some leftover pieces. It's not going to win any beauty contests, that's for sure. But piecrusts don't have to be pretty. They have to taste good.

"Do you want to add the filling, or should I do it?" I ask.

"Go ahead," Maribel says, not looking up from her phone.

Carefully, I pour the strawberries into the pan. I let out a deep breath. Not bad. Now that the lumpy crust is mostly covered, it looks like a real pie—maybe even a good one. I slide the pan into the oven and set the timer.

I push the dough scraps into the trash, then wash the rolling pin by hand. The whole time, I replay our conversation, trying to figure out exactly where things went wrong.

As the minutes pass, the whole kitchen begins to smell

delicious. I guess it's hard to go wrong with butter, fruit, and flour—even if it is gluten-free flour.

After a few moments, Maribel looks up from what she's doing. "Why is Griffin Connor so important to you anyway?"

"Besides the fact he's the biggest influence on my cooking?" I ask. "I guess it's because he's brilliant."

She snorts. "That's debatable."

"He's so confident," I say. "Everyone listens to him. Everyone loves his food."

She drums her fingers on the countertop. "Maybe he can cook. But . . . he's basically a terrible person, right? Or he acts like one for the cameras anyway. Like when he throws muffins at people and calls them names."

Just the thought of it makes me snicker. "*Muffinhead, Muffinhead!* It's hilarious."

She shrugs. "And you said he thinks recipes are for losers? That's not nice. How are people supposed to learn how to cook?"

I roll my eyes. "They're *supposed* to watch his videos. That's the best way to learn."

Maribel sniffs. "Or the best way to keep his website views up."

"That's unfair. His website helps people. Like me, for example. I used to cook with my best friend Malcolm's mom—but after they moved away, I switched to Griffin Connor," I tell her.

Maribel shrugs. Clearly, she's not interested. She picks up her phone, and her fingers begin to fly. She's probably texting everyone she knows to tell them about our argument. The thought makes a lump form in my stomach—one roughly the size and shape of a piecrust.

The ticking of the kitchen timer fills the room. I start cleaning the dishes and wiping the counters. I'm grateful for something to do.

When the kitchen timer beeps, I breathe a sigh of relief. Maribel sets down her phone and smiles at me. It's a truce, for the moment anyway.

I hand her the pot holders. "Do you want to do the honors?"

Maribel pulls out the pie pan and sets it on the trivet.

The pie looks beautiful. The crust is golden. The strawberries are like rubies, shiny and perfect.

"Should we wait for it to cool?" I ask.

Maribel grins. "No way!"

I'm just happy to see her smile. I take a knife and make a cut. The knife glides through the strawberries easily. But when it hits the crust, it stops moving. I push the blade against the crust, but it's completely solid—like trying to slice a brick wall.

I try again, from a different angle—but no luck. "This isn't working."

Maribel holds out her hand. "Let me try."

I hand her the knife. She pushes down, but it's no use. The crust—*my* crust—is uncuttable.

"Let's at least try to eat the filling," she says. We each grab a spoon and scoop out some of the berries onto our plates.

It's steaming hot. After it cools a bit, I take a bite. The strawberries are sweet and tart. Adding the vanilla was a good idea—it adds complexity and depth.

"This filling is pretty good," she says.

"It's *really* good," I say. My voice sounds miserable. I know defeat when I see it—when I taste it. Maribel did so much better than I did.

She elbows me in the arm. "You don't have to sound so sad about it."

"My crust is terrible. We can't even cut it!"

Maribel shrugs. She reaches over and tries to break a piece of crust, but it won't budge. She bends it back and forth until a section snaps off. Eventually, she manages to break it in two.

I look at the crust in my hand. What I thought was golden brown now looks hard and greasy.

I watch Maribel. For once in my life, I'm hoping that I was wrong. It would take some kind of miracle, but maybe the crust will somehow be amazing.

Maribel chews. And chews. And chews some more. Finally, she swallows with a loud gulp.

Then she coughs, waving a hand near her throat. "Need . . . water."

I pour her a glass. The crust I'm holding feels like cardboard. It probably tastes like cardboard too. I better find out.

I put it in my mouth, but I can barely eat it. It's like my teeth are breaking off. I finally manage to swallow.

My stomach clenches. I'm supposed to be *good* at this—the kitchen is the one place where I don't mess up. And yet. This pie is a total disaster.

"I thought it would work," I say. "Usually cooking comes easy to me."

She shrugs, adding another scoop of filling onto her plate. I do the same. Even though it pains me to admit it, Maribel's strawberries are a raging success. I eat another bite.

Maribel pokes at the edge of the crust. "Maybe next time you should use a recipe."

A *recipe*! I push away my plate. I don't even want to look at it. Griffin Connor's face flashes in my mind, and all the strawberries turn sour in my stomach. This is the one place in the world where I never feel like a failure. And now I feel like the world's biggest Muffinhead.

Something twists inside me. Something mean.

"This is sort of your fault," I say.

Maribel stops chewing. "How so?"

"Admit it, some things are not meant to be gluten-free."

She flinches. I can almost hear a voice in the distance trying to warn me—one that says, *Nooo, Elliott. Negatory. Take it back, abort mission, eighty-six that idea because it's going to land you in some seriously hot water*—but I'm too upset, and besides, the thing about distant voices is that it's easy to ignore them, if you really want to. And I do.

"You know the filling is the easy part. It's the crust that's the actual work," I say.

Maribel's mouth drops open. "You told me *you* wanted to do the crust."

"I was trying to be nice," I answer. "Obviously, I'm way more experienced with cooking, so I didn't want you to have the hard part. No offense."

No offense. The words make me stop in my tracks. I sound like Victor and Gilbert and Kunal and Drew. I sound even worse. What am I *doing?*

Maribel is already across the room. She grabs her notebook and heads for the front door.

"Wait," I say. "Maribel—"

But she heads out the door. Her parents' car is in the driveway. She gets in the back seat, and they drive away.

Maribel Martinez is gone. And I feel like the biggest Muffinhead of all.

CHAPTER 22

On Monday, Maribel doesn't speak to me for the entire Advisory period. I try a few times, but she won't even look at me. Eventually, I give up.

Tuesday afternoon, I walk to Dr. Gilmore's. Inside his office, I flop on the yellow sofa.

"Do you want to play a game?" he asks.

"Nah," I say.

"Okay," he says.

I slouch down in my seat. All I can think of is the project, which is definitely going to be a total disaster.

Dr. Gilmore waits to see if I am going to say more, but I keep my mouth shut. I cross my arms tight and slouch even lower.

But finally, I can't stand the silence.

"Maribel and I made a pie for our project. Her part of the pie came out great, but my crust was terrible," I say. "I'm supposed to be good at cooking! And pies are supposed to be easy. I don't know why it didn't turn out."

Dr. Gilmore tilts his head. "Who says that pies are easy?"

"Griffin Connor," I say. Dr. Gilmore knows how I feel about *Cheftastic!*

"Ah," Dr. Gilmore says. "Does Griffin Connor make many pies?"

I groan, covering my eyes with my hands. "He says they're too simple. He says baked goods don't elevate the palate."

Dr. Gilmore snorts. "That's one way to get out of doing something. Just say that it's too easy and then never do it."

I lower my hands. "What did you say?"

"He's the one who doesn't use recipes, right?" Dr. Gilmore asks. "Why do you think that is?"

"So people learn how to be like a real chef," I say.

Dr. Gilmore rubs the back of his neck thoughtfully. "Okay. But you know what? Sometimes it's okay to use a recipe. Sometimes it's okay to say you don't know how to do something and then learn to do it, step-by-step."

I cross my arms. I don't want to talk about this anymore.

"Recipes are fine for some people but not for me," I say. "I'm supposed to be good at everything in the kitchen."

"That sounds like a lot of pressure," Dr. Gilmore says mildly.

I shrug. "Maybe, but you know I'm serious about cooking. Besides, I don't know if I said anything that bad. The last time a baker visited *Cheftastic!*, Griffin Connor kept making jokes about how baking wasn't as hard as cooking. No one got mad at him."

Dr. Gilmore raises his eyebrows.

I sigh. "Well, I say *jokes*, but the baker didn't seem to find it all that funny. She actually walked out. They put it with funny music, and I thought it seemed funny at the time, but maybe it wasn't. Not to her anyway."

"Hmm," Dr. Gilmore says.

"I know what you're going to say," I tell him. "You think I should tell Maribel that I'm sorry."

Dr. Gilmore smiles. "The important thing is that *you* seem to think you should. That's worth thinking about."

Before I know it, the time is up. It's weird. Sometimes it seems like Dr. Gilmore doesn't talk very much, but it's in those sessions where it feels like the most gets said.

I grab a peppermint from Ms. Jolene's desk and turn to go, but I bump right into someone.

I step backward, about to say *excuse me*, but then I realize that it's Dad.

"Hey," he says, catching me. "Easy there."

"But Mom's picking me up today," I say. "Why are you here?"

"Oh," Dad says. "Well—"

"Mark," a woman calls from the door to the back offices.

"I'll explain later," Dad says. "See you Friday."

He turns to follow the person through the doors to the back office. Probably it's a billing question or some scheduling thing.

I step outside into the afternoon sunshine. I'm supposed to meet Mom at the library at 4:30 p.m., so I start making my way back through the shops toward the center of town.

As I walk, it starts to sprinkle so I pull up my hood. I don't mind the rain. As I get closer to the library though, it starts coming down harder. I duck underneath the awning for Sugar Rose. Even out here on the sidewalk, I can smell the sweet, yeasty doughnuts. I turn to look in their window, and there's a face looking out at me—it's Kunal. He raises his hand in a wave.

I push open the door and go inside. Kunal sits on a stool with a half-finished math worksheet in front of him. He also has a paper plate with three doughnuts on it.

I slide onto the seat next to him. "Hey. What are you doing here?"

He tilts his head in the direction of the counter. "Waiting for my cousin."

Behind the display case is a college-age-looking guy. He's filling a box for an older woman wearing a yellow raincoat.

"What about you?" he asks.

"Uh—" I start to say. Going to therapy is not a bad thing, but it's not something I really want to share. "I'm meeting my mom later, so I'm just hanging out."

Kunal tilts his head at the doughnuts on the table. "Want some of these?"

Without waiting for an answer, he picks up a plastic knife and starts cutting the doughnuts in pieces.

He pushes the plate in my direction, pointing to each of the doughnuts as he speaks. "Maple–Black Pepper, Raspberry–Corn Bread, Banana-Coconut."

Banana-Coconut has swirls of yellow and white icing with toasted coconut shreds. Raspberry–Corn Bread has powdered sugar on top. Maple–Black Pepper has a crumb topping with pepper sprinkled in.

I reach for the Maple–Black Pepper—because crumb toppings are the best—and take a huge bite. It's sweet but with a surprising kick to it.

"This is so good!"

Kunal grins. "That one's my favorite."

I take another bite, chewing more slowly this time.

We're quiet as I sample the other flavors. The others are good but not as delicious as the first. It's the crumb topping that makes that one stand out. The texture melts in my mouth, absolutely full of flavor—and butter. Someone should invent a doughnut made entirely out of crumbs.

Kunal has an earbud in, so I'm not sure if he's listening to music or if he wants to talk—but after a while, it feels awkward to sit here without saying *something*.

"How's the catapult project?" I ask.

Kunal makes a *pfffft* sound. "So far it's mostly lots of fighting over the design. Victor wants it to be more authentic, but Drew says we should simplify it so we can make a greater quantity. Gilbert doesn't care as long as we get an A."

My eyebrows pop up. Fighting? I hadn't noticed any tension at lunch. But sometimes I miss things.

"I know what you mean," I tell him. "Maribel and I tried working on our project last weekend, but it turned out bad."

Kunal looks interested. "What happened?"

I chew another bite of doughnut, thinking. "I guess it was just my part that turned out bad. Her part came out fine—really good, even. But now she's mad because of something I said."

Kunal sighs. "Group projects—I guess there's always something. Teachers act like they are supposed to help you learn to get along with others, but that's not that easy to do when a grade is at stake."

"Yeah," I say quietly. I'm thinking about how they didn't want me in their group.

Kunal looks at me sideways. "It wasn't right that we left you out. But you aren't missing much."

I don't know if I agree. No group is perfect, but being excluded is worse. But I appreciate that he said something instead of just ignoring it the way most people would. I want Kunal to be my friend. So I shrug like it's no big deal.

"Yeah," I say finally. "I kind of get it. Sometimes I mess stuff up."

Kunal nods. "Everyone messes up sometimes."

Something about his expression reminds me of the times with Malcolm, when I'd goof up in sports and he'd say *No big deal*. I grin and Kunal grins back.

We hang out for a while longer—eating our doughnuts, looking out the window, drinking ice water from paper cups. Eventually, it's time to meet Mom at the library, so I say goodbye.

Outside, it's still raining. I narrowly avoid getting smacked with an umbrella as I hurry to the crosswalk.

In some ways, this project would have been easier if I were working with Kunal and those guys. In a big group, I can float along a little more. That's harder to do when I'm working with just one other person.

But maybe working with one other person is good in other ways. Honestly, I could probably learn a lot from Maribel. She's organized. Thorough. She says whatever's on her mind.

Maribel. My stomach thuds. We were getting along pretty well until the baking disaster. But now we aren't speaking.

It seems like I need to do two things to get our project back on track.

One, figure out that piecrust.

Two, get Maribel to talk to me again.

Not necessarily in that order.

CHAPTER 23

When Advisory starts, I'm ready.

"Maribel, can we go to one of the coworking areas? I really want to talk about what happened," I say.

"Okay," she says finally.

When we find a spot by the window, she sits down. The expression on her face makes me think I might have a chance—but only one.

I clear my throat. "Maribel, I'm sorry about what happened at my house. I don't have an excuse for it. But it wasn't anything you did. I think—well, I *know*—that I was flustered and embarrassed because things weren't turning out how I thought they would. But I shouldn't have acted the way I did."

Maribel looks like she's thinking it over.

I take a deep breath. "And I am super, extra, especially sorry about making a big deal out of the gluten-free stuff. That was wrong."

She's quiet for a while. My insides bubble with nervousness. But eventually, she nods.

"Okay," she says. "But don't do it again."

I grin. "Okay!"

Maribel pulls out her pink gel pen. "Grab a seat, Elliott. We have a lot of work to do."

She slides the three-ring binder so it's on the table between us. As she flips the pages I feel like I'm seeing my life pass before my eyes. Or at least, my life for the next few weeks as we follow all her charts, diagrams, and figures.

Maribel points to a page titled Expenses. "Did you bring that receipt for the strawberries? Ms. Choi said we don't have to track items we already have around, like the vanilla from your pantry. But we'll definitely have to record the strawberries since they're perishable."

Miraculously, I remembered it. I dig in my pocket until I find the paper, then I smooth out most of the crumples.

I hand her the receipt. "They were local, from the farmers' market."

Maribel looks at the total, her eyes widening. "They're also super *expensive*."

"There was a late freeze, so there aren't as many local berries this year," I say, remembering what they said at the stand. "That's why the farmers have to charge more for the ones they have."

"Supply and demand," Maribel mutters through clenched teeth. She grabs a different gel pen—purple, this time—and jots down a few numbers.

When she looks back up, she is gnawing her lip. "That one pie took *four cups* of strawberries. Two pints, just for one pie."

"Okay," I say, not getting why she's so upset. "So we will buy two pints for each pie."

Maribel shakes her head. "There's a hundred-dollar budget for the entire project. So that means we could make around eight pies. Maybe ten, if we skimp on the berries."

Finally, I understand. "There's no way I'll make enough money that way."

"Not to mention our grade," Maribel says. "I don't think eight pies is enough."

We stare at the page together. It seems hopeless.

"Maybe there's another way to make it work," Maribel suggests. "I know that gluten-free flour is more expensive than regular."

She's right—it would be less money if we used wheat flour. But there's no way I could do that to her—especially after what I said last weekend.

"Nope," I say. "These pies will be gluten-free no matter what. It's nonnegotiable."

A smile bolts across her face. "Thanks, Elliott."

"Maybe the strawberries at the grocery store cost less than the farmers' market," I say. "Even if they aren't local."

Maribel looks unsure. "The directions say to buy local whenever possible."

"Maybe we should go to the grocery store and see if we can figure it out? Maybe if we buy everything from the Avery Market, it will still count as working with a local business? And they buy things local whenever they can."

Maribel sighs. "I know it's not as strong a connection as it could be, but maybe we don't have a choice."

"Don't worry," I say. "We'll figure out the strawberries, and we'll figure out the piecrust."

Maribel smiles. "Together."

"Together," I say firmly.

On the inside, I'm not so sure. But we better figure out something.

CHAPTER 24

Maribel's after-school schedule is, unsurprisingly, much busier than mine.

Between her volleyball and all her various activities (who even knew that ASG has a juggling club?) and my schedule going back and forth to Dad and Kate's and seeing Dr. Gilmore, it takes a while to find a time when we can both go to Avery Market. But eventually that day comes, and I'm waiting for Maribel on the school steps.

"Hi," she says when she sees me. She holds up a baggie of apple slices. "Do you want some of these?"

"Sure."

She gives me a handful, and we start walking toward downtown. I'm already feeling excited to go to Avery Market, which is sort of a combination of a grocery store and a convenience store. Half of the aisles are local, artisanal foods. And the other half are prepared foods, easy meals for people to grab to heat up the rest of the way at home or even salads and sandwiches and wraps for lunches. And of course, the best thing about Avery Market: free samples.

"I went in yesterday and talked to the manager, Janiyah. She said that she might be able to help us. You've been there before, right?" I ask.

Maribel shakes her head.

"My mom and I started coming here a few years ago, right around the time I started getting into cooking," I say. "They have all these little specialty counters, and I used to like going around to see what they had each time. It got so that people would see me coming and make special things for me to try. I was a little kid, but I loved everything—even habanero herring over pickled salsa."

Maribel grimaces. "I'll have to take your word for it."

I shake my head. "Trust me, it's delicious."

We push open the front door and head for the customer service area. Behind the desk is Bailey, who has bright pink hair and a tattoo of a root beer float on their arm.

"Hi, Elliott," Bailey says. "I'll let Janiyah know you're here. Do y'all want to try these chips?"

I help myself to a handful of orange chips dotted with pumpkin seeds.

"Are they gluten-free?" Maribel asks. Bailey shows her the label, and Maribel reads it carefully before trying a few.

"It stinks that you have to double-check everything," I say.

She shrugs. "It's better than getting sick."

I nod. "That makes sense."

"But, yeah," she says. "It actually does stink. A lot."

Janiyah, the store manager, comes over to us. She is tall, and her hair is lots of long, skinny braids. She's holding a clipboard and has a huge smile. We say hi, and I introduce her to Maribel.

"Well, that's awesome that you two are working so hard on your project," she says. "And pies—what a great idea. Everyone loves pie."

"The only problem is that there isn't a lot of local fruit in season right now," Maribel says. "And strawberries cost so much."

"We were hoping that maybe we could get some kind of discount or something if we got them from you," I say.

Janiyah taps the clipboard. "The local crops were hit hard by a late frost. We just don't have a lot of wiggle room there. I'm sorry."

My shoulders slump. We're never going to figure out a way to make this project work.

"Is there another way we could help?" Janiyah asks. "What other ingredients do you need?"

Maribel and I exchange glances.

"We're still figuring out our crust," I admit.

"And the filling too," Maribel says.

"The one thing we know is that whatever we make has to be gluten-free," I say.

Janiyah brightens. "Let me show you our gluten-free section."

She walks us to a section in the back full of all kinds of things—cookies, crackers, pasta, bread, chips. Immediately, Maribel starts picking up boxes and reading labels.

"I'm going to have to come back here with my mom," she says excitedly.

Janiyah beams. "Great! Sorry we couldn't help with the berries. You two can feel free to use our community room if you need a place to talk things over. Elliott knows where it is."

We thank her, and she goes back to the front of the store.

"Now what?" I ask.

Maribel is totally focused on the box of macaroni and cheese she's holding.

"They have gluten-free *everything*," she whispers.

I sigh. As much as I am happy for her, we need to figure out our project. "Do you want to go to the community room?"

Maribel looks longingly at the box before setting it back on the shelf.

The store's community room is tucked in a corner of the store by the fresh flowers and juice bar. One wall has a big window that looks onto the street; the other wall has a window that looks back into the store. The other two walls are brick and lined with bookshelves. In the middle of the room is a long wooden table, which is surrounded by a variety of random-looking chairs. One side of the table has stacks of papers with coupons and flyers for upcoming events.

Maribel heads to the shelves immediately. "I've never seen so many cookbooks!" She traces their brightly colored spines with her finger.

I'm looking to see if they have any Griffin Connor titles when a low shelf catches my eye. It's crammed full, just like the other shelves. But unlike the other shelves with glossy hardcovers, these volumes are photocopies bound with plastic combs. Some are just papers folded in half and stapled.

I kneel for a better look. "What are these?"

Maribel takes a few from the shelf and pages through them.

"I think I know what these are," she says slowly. "I've seen this kind of thing at my grandma's house. They're community cookbooks. Fundraisers for churches and schools. Hers are all really old. I guess these are too."

I pick out a few. They're definitely old.[28]

Secrets from Our Kitchen, Avery Ladies' Society, 1972.

What's Cooking with Avery Community Church, 1968.

Our Favorite Recipes, The Willard School, 1981.

There's one without a year that just says *Delicious!*

---

[28] Mom would say *vintage* or *retro*, but we all know that means *old*.

I flip through the pages of a book with a pale pink cover. It's just text—there are no photos anywhere. "Were these made with . . . a *typewriter?*"

Maribel's eyes light up. "This is amazing! We might find a recipe that's an actual link to Avery's history."

Maribel and I sit crisscross with the towering stack of cookbooks between us. For a while, we're quiet except for the turning of pages.

Maribel flips through a cookbook with a tractor on the cover. "This one has eight different recipes for deviled eggs."

I turn the pages in mine. "This one has a whole *section* on Jell-O salads. Back then they sure used a lot of Cool Whip, cherries, and pecans."

Maribel shudders. "Not to mention cottage cheese."

"Pineapple-lime gelatin," I say. "I've had this at my grandma's house—it's my uncle Greg's favorite."

Maribel finds a book with a dessert section. "Look at this, *Pies of All Kinds*. That sounds promising. Pecan pie?"

"Nuts are expensive," I say.

"Apple pie?" she asks. "Pumpkin?"

"Out of season," I say.

I look at the pages along with her. Each of the recipes have names attached. It makes me wonder about who made the recipes and what their lives were like. Patty Halaney and her macaroni salad. Nancy Williams and her chicken casserole. Sarah Palmer and her stuffed mushrooms.

"It's all women," Maribel says. "I haven't seen any men's names—have you?"

I shake my head.

"It's kind of amazing," she says. "Back then, I bet it was a big deal for someone to share a recipe. You couldn't just look it up online."

She's right. As I read the recipes, I have the feeling that whoever wrote them was handing over something important—something precious, in a way.

"Cobblers, crisps, and crumbles," I say. "Apple Brown Betty and Blueberry Slump."

"Hummingbird Cake," Maribel says. "Lady Baltimore Cake. Where are all the pies?"

"Desperation Pie," I read out loud.

Maribel's eyes widen. "What's that?"

I show her the page. It's a simple recipe—piecrust, eggs, butter, sugar, and vinegar.

"I don't get it," Maribel says. "Vinegar?"

I shrug. "*Desperation?*"

Maribel's already pulling out her phone. "I'll search for it . . . okay, here it says that desperation pies are also known as make-do pies. It means that you make the most of what you have."

I scoot closer to see.

Desperation pies have been around at least since the 1700s.
They experienced a surge of popularity during the Great
Depression. They exist because of the ingenuity of home

bakers. There were times when it wasn't easy to get fresh fruit, but it was usually possible to keep the ingredients for these pies on hand.

Maribel looks thoughtful. "Technically, I think the one you found is called a vinegar pie. There are other desperation pies too—chess pie, buttermilk pie, mock apple pie."

She's scrolling faster than I can read. "Mock apple pie?"

"It's fake apple pie," Maribel says. "It's made with boiled crackers soaked in sugar."

"Agggh," I say. "That sounds disgusting."

Maribel shrugs. "Vinegar pie sounds kind of gross too, but this article says it's good."

I shudder. "Well, the cracker one is worse. Let's keep looking."

I reach for another cookbook. But Maribel is frowning.

"But, Elliott," she says. "Don't you see? If we make one of these pies, we won't have to use any of our budget to make them. They're all pantry ingredients. Maybe you could argue that we had to pay for the eggs, but that isn't very much money."

She rummages in her backpack, pulling out her binder and an orange gel pen. She flips to a blank page and starts scribbling.

"Let's say we spend less than a dollar per pie on eggs and the pie plate together. If we sell the pie for ten dollars, then we will make nine dollars per pie."

169

I close my eyes. I don't know if vinegar pie will be any good. But what if it is? At nine dollars per pie, we could sell a hundred pies and make nine hundred dollars—I would get half, which is almost everything I need to pay back Dad. Culinary camp, here I come. That's all I need to make up my mind.

I take out my phone and take a picture of the cookbook page. I'm going to actually use a recipe.[29]

"Let's do it," I say. "Desperation pie, here we come."

Maribel is grinning at me. She reaches over and nudges me with her pen.

"You know what this means," she says. "You have to learn how to make a decent crust."

"I'm on it," I say. I'll figure it out somehow. I have to.

---

[29] Somewhere in the distance, Griffin Connor sheds a silent tear. (In my imagination anyway.)

CHAPTER 25

When I call from the store, Mom says she can give Maribel a ride home. Maribel checks with her parents, and then we pile in Mom's car.

Maribel says her address, and Mom looks up the directions. Maribel lives on the other side of town.

Mom turns on her blinker and pulls away from the curb. "Were you able to work out a deal with the store?"

"Even better," Maribel says, and launches into an explanation about the cookbook room and the pies. I half listen and half watch the cars go by. Usually I'm shy around other people's parents, but Maribel isn't at all.

Mom listens and asks questions at the right times. She tilts her head. "Why are they called desperation pies?"

"It's because people made them when they were desperate," Maribel says. "They had to take what they had and make the most of it."

Mom grins. "Sounds like they had the right idea."

We turn right into a neighborhood with stone pillars at the entrance.

"It's going to be amazing, I just know it," Maribel says.

I start to wonder if this pie is such a good idea after all. It seemed like the perfect solution back in the storeroom, but maybe we were kidding ourselves. Who would ever think to put vinegar in a pie? Griffin Connor would probably throw that pie across the room.

"When are you going to make these desperation pies?" Mom asks.

"The sooner, the better," Maribel says.

In the rearview mirror I can see that Mom is smiling.

"That sounds like a plan," Mom says.

She starts to drive more slowly. The phone says, "You have arrived."

"There it is, the brick one on the right," Maribel says.

My eyebrows pop up. Maribel's house is huge. I think *house* might not even be the right word. I think Maribel's house is technically a mansion.

"Whoa," I say. "Nice place."

Maribel either doesn't hear me or she acts like she doesn't. "Thanks again for the ride. See you tomorrow, Elliott."

Mom waits to make sure Maribel gets inside okay—Mom does that with everyone. After Maribel opens the door, she turns and waves to us.

"She's a nice kid," Mom says. "I'm glad to see you're making more friends."

I roll my eyes. "Mom. We're just project partners."

But on the inside, I think that maybe Mom is right—Maribel might actually be a friend. The good news is, I need all the friends I can get. The bad news is, I don't want to let her down. I better figure out this piecrust problem fast.

CHAPTER 26

When we get home, I check on Denver and Omelet and then join Mom in the kitchen. She has the big pot on the stove and is thawing a batch of her homemade tomato soup—she freezes it in the summer so we can enjoy it all year.

"I'm making grilled cheese sandwiches tonight," she says. "How do you want yours—arugula, bacon, and fig jam? Brie, apple, and honey mustard? Cheddar and blackberry jelly?"

I sigh. "Whatever. It doesn't matter."

"Uh-oh." Mom turns to look at me sharply, then crosses the room and presses the back of her hand against my forehead.

I pull away. "What are you doing?"

Her eyebrows are furrowed in mock-concern. "I can't remember the last time you had no opinion about food. I figured you must be coming down with something."

"Ha ha," I say. "I'm okay. I'm just trying to figure out piecrust."

Mom tilts her head sideways. "Well, in that case, can you caramelize some onions for us? You know I always burn them to a crisp."

I nod. "It's true—you do."

Mom throws a dish towel at me. "Hey!" she says in pretend-outrage.

I shrug. "You said it; I was just agreeing with you."

She laughs. I grab three onions, cut the roots and stems off, and then start slicing lengthwise. Then, I warm the big pan before adding olive oil and butter.

Mom spreads mayo onto the outsides of the bread slices—her secret ingredient for making grilled cheese sandwiches. "You've taken on big cooking challenges before. What's so different this time?"

"The problem is that it's a *baking* project," I say. "Baking has so many rules that I don't understand. I want it to be easier."

Mom's eyes crinkle in a smile. "Sometimes things are worth doing even if they aren't easy. *Especially* if they aren't easy."

I stare gloomily at my onions. "I guess."

Mom pats my arm. "You'll figure it out—I promise."

Griffin Connor probably doesn't ever feel stuck like this.

In the pan, my onions start to turn pale brown. The entire caramelization process takes a long time—at least thirty minutes. I want them to turn rich and brown but not black and burned.

As I watch, my brain does that thing where it is thinking about lots of things at once.

The light brown color reminds me of the Maple–Black Pepper doughnut at Sugar Rose. Those crumbs on top were so good. I remember thinking that it would be good if there was a way to make an entire doughnut out of crumbs.

After about ten minutes, I sprinkle the onions with salt and also add a teaspoon of sugar to help things along.

There's a real trick to caramelization. If I stir too much, they won't brown. But if I leave them too long without stirring, they'll burn.

I keep thinking about that doughnut—the flavor and the texture were so well balanced. Sweet and smooth, spicy and warm, melting in my mouth. Even as I was chewing, I couldn't wait to take another bite. That's the kind of food I want to make.

And then it hits me—a brand-new idea. I'm so excited that I almost drop my spatula. Maybe there's a way to take the best parts of a crumb topping and the best parts of the crust and put them together. Something that will save our pies, make Maribel happy, and help me pay back Dad. That isn't too much to ask from a piecrust, is it?

PART FOUR

Desperation Pie

EGGS, VINEGAR, BROWN SUGAR, BUTTER

Better than
it looks

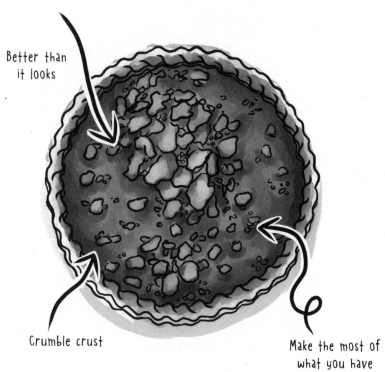

Crumble crust

Make the most of
what you have

CHAPTER 27

After school, Maribel's mom picks us up. Her name is Carla, and she looks a lot like Maribel, except that her hair is in a ponytail instead of a braid.

Maribel's house doesn't feel formal like I thought it might from the outside. Inside it's friendly looking, with a big staircase and white walls with lots of paintings on the wall and pottery everywhere. Carla says she has some work to do and goes upstairs to her office.

"Come on," Maribel says. "Let's get a snack."

The kitchen is enormous—even bigger than Dad and Kate's. It's got an island that seats eight, double ovens, and two sinks—but I can't take my eyes off the gleaming professional range with a giant exhaust hood.

"Does your family like to cook?" I ask.

"Not really," Maribel says.

I shake my head. "If I had this kitchen, I'd never want to leave."

"It's too big," she says. "I like yours better."

Before I can answer, Maribel pulls open a door—I thought it was a cabinet, but it's really a refrigerator. "Do you want a snack?"

Without waiting for an answer, she emerges with a bunch of grapes and a mesh bag full of little wax-wrapped cheeses. She heads into her pantry—which is an actual room that she can stand inside of—and comes back with some crackers and cookies.

"They're gluten-free," she says. "Everything is."

"Does your family have celiac too?" I ask.

She grabs two plates from a drawer. "No, I'm the only one."

I arrange my food on the plate. I think about telling Maribel about my Legendary Snack Bowls, but I'm not sure if that would be a weird thing to say.

The kitchen is quiet except for the sound of us chewing. I feel like maybe I did something to make her mad.

"Hey," I say. "I have an idea for the piecrust."

This makes her smile. "Is it an *idea*, or did you actually consult a recipe?"

Okay, maybe I deserved that.

"It started as an idea, but then I looked up some recipes."

She raises an eyebrow.

"I was thinking about the cobblers and crisps that were in one of the community cookbooks, and I thought—I like those crumbles better than a regular old piecrust anyway. So I thought we could try making a different kind of crust—a crumble crust."

I open my backpack and show her the ingredients. "I saw a recipe that uses almond meal and sugar."

Maribel looks skeptical. "We would have to label it carefully so no one with a nut allergy eats it accidentally."

"Let's just try it," I say. "At this point, there's nothing to lose."

I wash my hands while Maribel gets out measuring cups, pie pans, and bowls. I realize that Maribel's house is quiet—too quiet.

"Do you mind if we turn some music on or something?" I ask.

"Sure," she says. She taps on her phone, and soon electronic music comes from speakers that are tucked up underneath the cabinets. "Is this okay?"

"It's great—when it's silent, I can't think," I say.

Maribel turns on the water and starts scrubbing her hands. "Is that an ADHD thing?"

"That's what Dr. Gilmore says," I blurt out without thinking.

Maribel looks up. "Who's that?"

"He's, uh, someone my parents make me go see every week. To talk to," I say.

"Oh," says Maribel. "You mean a therapist?"

I freeze. I don't know any kids who talk about going to therapy.

"It's not a big deal, Elliott. I had to see one too, after I got diagnosed with celiac," she says. "It took a long time to figure out what was wrong with me. My stomach hurt all the time, and I had these headaches. We tried eliminating a lot of things, but then we found out it was gluten. I felt better almost right away."

I tilt my head, thinking. Part of me can't believe how open Maribel is about going to therapy. The other part of me can't understand why she ever had to go in the first place. She seems to have everything in life figured out.

"I don't get it," I say finally. "If you were feeling better, then why did you have to go to therapy?"

She takes out a whisk and starts beating the eggs, quiet for a while before answering.

"This is the thing about celiac disease," she says finally. "I might look like everyone else on the outside, but on the inside, I'm different. My body can't process gluten without getting really sick. What's easy for other people isn't so easy for me."

"I never thought about it like that," I say. "That's true for me and ADHD. It's not really something that you could tell just by looking at me—but my insides are different too."

Maribel nods. "I was really upset when I got diagnosed. First, I didn't know why it took them so long to figure it out.

I mean, my parents are both doctors. But then I was just depressed because there are so many things that I can't eat. And mad! I was so mad, almost all the time."

I think back to what I said on our first day working together—the way I reacted when I realized Maribel wanted everything to be gluten-free. She was so mad. It makes sense now.

I clear my throat. "I'm sorry about what I said. I didn't understand."

"Thanks," she says. "But those kinds of comments happen a lot. I'm tired of celiac disease being a punch line. Sometimes when someone finds out I can't have gluten they act like it's a joke, or they even get mad at me. I want to say—'I can't help it. I wish I could eat whatever I wanted. I'd give anything to change this part of myself'—you know?"

"I *do* know," I say, thinking of my ADHD.

But I don't know if I would make my brain different if I could. There are a lot of things I don't like about my ADHD—sometimes I *hate* it. But it's also a part of me. If I altered that part of my brain, would it also mean that I wouldn't cook like I do now? I don't know.

"Mostly, I wish I could be better at math. It's really hard to focus on numbers,"[30] I say.

Maribel sighs happily. "Oh, I'm the opposite. I *love* math.

[30] It's like my brain has a nonstick coating when it comes to numbers—they just slip right out.

It's like learning a language, in a way—a language full of numbers and letters and every time the answer is the same."

I shake my head. Leave it to Maribel to get excited about math.

She tilts her head, looking at me. "Did something specific happen for you to go to therapy? Or did you just decide to go one day?"

My throat feels tight. The truth: I don't want to talk about it. The other truth: maybe I actually do.

My cheeks are hot. I can't even get the words out; I just shake my head back and forth.

"You don't have to tell me," Maribel says. "I know I ask a lot of questions."

"I'll tell you," I say. "I just—I'm not used to talking about it. But I call it The Incident."

"Hold on," Maribel says. "I need to sit down for this." She pulls up a chair, like she's settling in.

My palms feel sweaty, but I figure I better start talking before I change my mind.

"It happened the day that Dad and Kate told me that they're having a baby."

Maribel's eyes widen. "Wait, you're getting a half brother soon?"

"Yeah," I say. I'm kind of expecting her to make a big deal about it, and I realize this is a sexist thing to say, but I guess I just assume that most girls like babies. So I'm surprised when she makes a gross-out face.

"Ugh," she says. "I would *not* be excited about a new baby brother or sister right now. And also: yuck. No offense to your dad and Kate."

I laugh. "Yeah. No offense taken. So anyway, they told me. And I guess they thought I'd be excited, but I got really quiet. It was like there were a gazillion feelings bubbling around inside me and I didn't know how to get them out."

I check her expression, because I don't know if she might think that sounds silly or immature, but she just nods sympathetically.

"So my dad—he's really into these father-son-type moments—he kept saying, 'Come on, Elliott. Let's go play some baseball in the yard.' Which, I don't even like baseball, so I said no. But he kept asking, so eventually I said okay."

Maribel takes a bite of cheese. "Then what?"

"Then he got a call," I say. "A work call. And I was waiting in the yard for him, and I just got really mad. So I threw a baseball at the house. We had a whole bucket of them, so I was just throwing them at the house as hard as I could."

"Whoa," Maribel says.

My cheeks feel kind of warm, but I keep talking. "It's a brick house, so it's not like it would hurt it. Except one of the balls hit a window."

Maribel's eyebrows pop up. "Uh-oh."

"Exactly," I say. "But, uh, then I kept throwing the balls and ended up breaking that window in a few different places. On purpose. My dad was so mad."

"I bet," Maribel says.

"Then I started going to therapy. That's it," I say.

Maribel is quiet. I get a little nervous.

I clear my throat. "Do you think I'm a bad person or something?"

Maribel lets out a big breath. "Oh, no way. I mean, obviously—bad choice, right, Elliott? In a million years, no one would suggest breaking a window as a coping strategy. So therapy is probably a good idea. But it doesn't sound like it's the end of the world or anything."

I'm stunned. It feels like I revealed a deep secret and maybe it wasn't such a big deal after all. When I finally process the fact that she, somehow, is still my friend, I shake my head as if to clear it.

"*Coping strategy?*" I ask, stretching the words out. "You sound exactly like my therapist."

Maribel tilts her head sideways. "I think all of them say stuff like that. Techniques. Methods. Strategies."

I wrinkle my nose. "Yeah, but remembering *and* quoting it is another thing altogether."

Maribel laughs. "Of course I remember it! You thought my binder was big for *our* project. You should see my therapy binders."

My mouth drops open. "Wait a second. Did you say *binders*? Plural, as in more than one?"

She nods. "I'm very thorough."

I have no idea how to respond to this.

Maribel punches me in the arm. "Come on. Let's figure out this pie."

For a while, we just listen to the music as we work. It's a comfortable kind of quiet. When I get the crust together, I tilt the pan to show her. The crumbs are pale and golden, and they cover the surface completely.

She raises her eyebrows. "That looks pretty good."

"That filling looks pretty good too," I say. It's true.

She pours in the filling, and then I put the pie in the oven. I grab a few grapes that are left in the bowl. Maribel loads our dishes in the dishwasher.

"Do you want help?" I ask.

But Maribel shakes her head. "I have a specific way I like to load it. It's easier if I do it myself."

Maribel is quick and efficient, loading dishes in a fraction of the time it would take me to do it. Whatever her future career is, she is probably going to be good at it. I have this feeling that she'll carry a special three-ring binder or at least a clipboard.

"Are you going to be a doctor like your parents?" I ask.

Maribel stares at me. At first, I think it's because my brain did an ADHD-jump and changed topics. But then I realize that her expression isn't surprised. She's *horrified*. She looks exactly like I would look if someone added some fat, juicy slugs on top of my Legendary Snack Bowl.

"Absolutely not! What makes you say that?"

I break into a sweat. "Oh, uh. Because you said your parents are, I guess? And you . . . seem to be good at lots of stuff."

Maribel snorts. "My parents are both brain surgeons. My brother is a brain surgeon. My sister is—hold on, because this is really shocking—a *heart* surgeon. So when I tell them I want to go into business, they don't want to hear it. They think it's a passing phase. It's really annoying."

"My dad thinks cooking is a waste of time," I say. "He says it will never pay the bills."

"If you want it to, it will," she says. "The key with dads is to show them how well you can do something. That's why this project is so good—you'll show your dad how much money you earn by making food."

The timer buzzes, and Maribel puts on pot holders. She opens the door and peeks in. "Oooh! They're done."

She sets them on a rack to cool. They're brown on the top and look kind of plain. I can't help feeling disappointed.

"They're kind of basic, huh?"

Maribel laughs. "Elliott, they are literally the most basic pie ever. They're made from whatever people had in their pantry when they had almost no food left."

"Okay, okay," I say. "I just thought they'd look a little better."

"Be more worried about how they taste," she says.

We wait for them to cool, and it's torture. They smell a lot better than they look. Finally, it's time to cut them open.

"Look at that," Maribel says. "They're bright yellow. Is that pretty enough for you, Elliott?"

"Much better," I say. "I approve."

We blow on our pieces to cool them faster. I lift my fork to my mouth.

"Wait!" Maribel says. "Let's try it at the exact same time. On three, ready?"

"One, two, three," we say together.

I take a bite. It's still hot. But already I can tell that it's warm and tender and buttery and sweet.

I wipe my mouth. "This . . . is really good."

Maribel hugs herself in happiness. "It's amazing. The crust is so good too, Elliott—it's almost like a cookie. I can't believe this is gluten-free!"

We finish our pieces. I scrape the plate to get all the crumbs.

Maribel is doing the same thing.

We push our plates to the side.

Maribel pulls out her binder. "All right," she says. "Now let's get to work."

We look at the binder for a while. Maribel worked on our budget some more. I wrote a paragraph about the history of desperation pies.

After an hour, we decide that we might need to test out the pie again. We cut another piece for each of us.

I may not ever be the biggest fan of spreadsheets, but I think most things are better with a slice of pie on the side.

CHAPTER 28

I'm looking out the window and thinking about pie.

"Elliott?" Dr. Gilmore says. "Distracted today?"

I look back at the game board—it's my turn, but I hadn't noticed. I wonder how much time has passed since I was supposed to go. But Dr. Gilmore never gets annoyed when I'm thinking about other things.

"I was just thinking about the pie project," I say.

Dr. Gilmore leans back in his chair. "How's that going?"

"Really good," I say. I update him on the new crust recipe and tell him all about the desperation pie.

He wrinkles his nose. "Vinegar pie? Really?"

"It's good, I promise!" I say. "I'll bring you one."

"I'd like that," Dr. Gilmore says.

I pick up one of the game pieces—I don't really remember the rules to this game anyway—and start flipping it over, trying to find its balance point. It's made of wood and feels smooth in my hand.

I take a deep breath. "So Maribel asked about my therapy. She said she goes too, sometimes. And she asked why I started going, but you know—I don't like to talk about The Incident."

Dr. Gilmore nods. "Did she understand that you don't like to talk about it?"

"She did," I say. "But, I kind of wanted to tell her. So . . . I did."

I glance at Dr. Gilmore. He's grinning.

"What was that like?" he asks.

"It was good, actually," I say. "Don't get me wrong—it was *hard*. I was worried she would think I was a bad person. But after I did it, I felt better."

"Have you talked with any of your other friends about it?" he asks.

I shake my head. "If Malcolm still lived here, I would talk to him. But not the guys I have lunch with—that's not the kind of thing we talk about."

"There are all different kinds of friends," Dr. Gilmore says. "Some friends are talking friends. Some friends are more *doing* friends."

I think about my time at Maribel's house. We made pie and we worked on our project together. We also talked a lot.

"I think Maribel might be both," I say.

Dr. Gilmore smiles so wide that his eyes crinkle up. "Then you're lucky—that's rare."

I nod.

"Do you want to tell me about that day with the window? Sometimes it's good to practice," Dr. Gilmore says.

I wait for my hands to get sweaty, but it doesn't happen. There's a lump in my stomach, but it's miniature-sized. I can talk around it. I remember exactly how I felt that day when Dad took that call instead of staying with me. It was cold, and my hands were stinging. I smelled fireplace smoke from some other house in the neighborhood. A place where a family was probably having hot chocolate or reading or playing games—all together.

"The sound of the glass felt so loud. But no one came to check on me," I say. "So I threw another ball and then another. Until Dad came outside and made me stop."

I put my head in my hands.

Dr. Gilmore tilts his head. "It seems like you feel really bad about it."

"I do," I say, not looking up.

"People make mistakes sometimes," Dr. Gilmore says.

I take off my glasses and wipe them on my shirt.

But then something weird happens. I start talking about other things.

About making a scene with Dad and Kate at dinner when I spilled my Coke. About our talk at the City River.

I even tell him about the new baby getting the same middle name as Dad and me—and how unfair that is.

And before I know it, Dr. Gilmore is saying, "That's almost all the time we have for today."

My eyebrows pop up. "Really?"

I look at the clock, which looks right back at me like it's saying, *Yeah—really.*

I can't believe how fast our session went by.

"That was good work, Elliott," Dr. Gilmore says. "How do you feel after talking about all of that?"

I look at the Mad, Sad, Brave, Calm words painted on his wall.

I squinch up my forehead, thinking. "I guess I feel . . . mostly tired?"

Dr. Gilmore chuckles. "You worked hard—that was a lot."

I grab my backpack and head for the door. But I notice that my chest isn't squeezing. My face isn't hot. I do feel mad about some things—and sad about others. But I also feel brave and calm. I'm all of them at once, which I guess is the way it happens sometimes with feelings.

CHAPTER 29

A funny thing happened after talking with Dr. Gilmore—I felt better.

Not *better* in the way of being a hundred percent perfect. But better than before.

In a way, it reminds me of being a little kid visiting the playground with the rocket slide. Every time it seemed like a piece of mulch would find its way inside my shoe. I never stopped to fix it because obviously I was busy pretending to be an astronaut. But every time, just before we left the playground, Mom would make me shake out the dirt. When I put my shoes on again, I noticed how roomy and comfortable they felt.

Don't get me wrong—I'm not proud of it. I feel bad

about what happened, and I definitely wish I hadn't done it. But I'm not thinking of it as The Incident anymore. Maybe just the incident, with lowercase letters. I can even imagine a time where I might not even call it that. Instead, it will be the time I broke that window. The time I made a mistake. Maybe it's not the kind of thing that needs to have its own special title.

After all, I told Maribel, and she still wants to be my friend. I told Dr. Gilmore, and he said that everyone makes mistakes sometimes. Something has shifted, and it's impossible not to notice.

This coming weekend Dad and Kate are planning a weekend vacation out to Gingerbread Island—a getaway for the two of them before the baby comes. This is fine by me, because the one time I went there I was totally bored. I am not what you'd call a beach person. Besides, the water is freezing this time of year anyway. I mean, okay, there is a good ice cream place and I do like fresh fish. But I've never been into the idea of trying to catch one myself.

Dad says that we should go to dinner that Thursday before they leave—just him and me—and I say okay. So that's how we end up at the Lebanese place we love for dinner. We order our favorite things, and I remind Dad to get a to-go order of the turnip pickles for Kate. Everything's actually going okay until I mention Maribel.

Dad gets this weird smile on his face. "Tell me about Maribel. Do you *like* her?"

My face gets warm. I know what he's saying—he doesn't mean "like her" in a friend way. He means do I *like* her. In a *Do-you-think-she's-pretty?* kind of way.

Dad laughs. "If you're quiet, that means you like her. I knew it!"

I scowl at my chicken shawarma. "Dad, no. I don't like anyone like that."

He spears a piece of lettuce. "You can't fault me for asking, Elliott. I know that I started to notice girls when I was your age."

"She's my friend," I say. "That's all. Please don't embarrass me at the festival. It's not like I have a whole lot of friends to replace her if you make it awkward between us."

Dad sets down his fork. "I didn't mean to upset you— I just wanted to know."

I take a bite of shawarma. "Now you know."

He folds his hands. "What did you mean about not having a lot of friends?"

I shrug, still chewing.

"It's been hard since Malcolm left, huh?" Dad asks.

A burst of irritation sparks inside me. It's like Dad hasn't been paying attention to my life this entire year.

I take a gulp from my water glass. "Let's see, best friend leaving right before starting a new school and then almost failing first semester? Yeah, you could say it's been hard."

Dad nods thoughtfully. "A lot has happened this year. New school, new brother, having to find new friends. Is there something I can do to help?"

196

At first, I want to say no. I want to show him how mad I am that he hasn't been paying attention to my life.

But then I think for a moment. Dad's voice sounded so tentative—probably because we aren't used to talking about feelings. But I'm glad he is trying. Maybe I can try too.

"I can't solve it," Dad says. "I'm not trying to. I'm just asking if there's one small thing I could do that would make a difference."

I slurp my Coke and then wipe my mouth. *"Kingdom of Krull."*

Dad scratches his head. "Kingdom of what?"

"Krull," I say. "That video game you and Mom said was too mature. My lunch friends play it, and that's all they talk about."

Dad's eyes narrow. "Maybe you should find new friends—friends who have other interests."

I sigh. "Dad, why did you ask me what would help if you were going to tell me that I'm wrong?"

Dad blinks, like he's surprised.

We're quiet like that for a while.

Then Dad looks sheepish. "I didn't think about it that way before. You're right, Elliott."

My eyes get so big I honestly think they might fall out of my head.

"I can't promise you the game," Dad clarifies. "But I'm going to consider it. And if this is the one thing that you want, well, your mom and I should take that seriously."

It feels like a trick. But Dad doesn't take it back. Not perfect, but trying. That's true for both of us.

CHAPTER 30

We're down to the last week before Avery Local. Maribel has an orthodontist appointment, so I know she won't be in Advisory—but that's okay. After all the hours we've worked, the project is perfectly on track.

Ms. Choi comes over to check on me. "Elliott, what are you going to work on? Do you want to join a different group for the day? Maybe you can help one another."

I look around the room. I could never admit this to Maribel, but I find myself missing her famous three-ring binder. I actually feel lost without it.

Ms. Choi drums her fingers on my desk. "You could work with Parker's group—they're also doing a baking project."

My eyes widen. Maribel would be furious if I shared information with Parker and the cupcake group.

"That's okay," I say quickly. "We are all set with the baking stuff. We're trying to figure out how to maximize how much money we make—I could work with any group to talk about that."

Ms. Choi's face brightens. "Why don't you go work with the catapult group? They're working on the same issue." She turns her head. "Gilbert's group, Elliott is going to work with you today."

Gilbert barely glances this way, but at least Kunal gives me a grin.

Ms. Choi gives me a little go-on wave and then turns to check in with Nate and Alex.

I pull up a chair to see what they're talking about. Having lunch together is one thing, but I'm not going to lie—it feels super awkward sitting with them as they work on the project they didn't want me on. But still, if it's a choice between Parker's group and these guys, I'd pick my lunch friends every time.

Victor and Drew are deep in a conversation about profit margins, which is the difference between how much something costs to make and how much you sell it for. It's math, so it's not my favorite—but it's something I've been thinking about. I guess Kunal's group has been thinking about it too.

I pick up one of their catapult prototypes and rotate it slowly so I can see how it's put together. Stacks of craft sticks are held together with rubber bands. A perpendicular stick has a spoon attached, which is where you put the thing you want to launch.

"This is pretty cool," I say.

"Don't mess with it," says Victor in a kind of snotty way.

"Sorry," I say, putting it back where it was.

Kunal frowns. "He isn't hurting it, Victor. Besides, we have about a hundred of them." He slides the prototype back onto my desk.

Victor rolls his eyes and goes back to talking with Drew.

Kunal shakes his head. "Don't worry about him. How's the baking going?"

"Not bad," I say.

"You should come by Sugar Rose again sometime," he says. "They have a new Meyer Lemon flavor that's really good."

"Okay," I say. "Maybe I will."

"*Hello*, Kunal, we need you here," says Drew. "How much do we think we can charge for these, realistically?"

"Maybe four dollars," Victor says. "At the very most."

Gilbert sighs. "I think four dollars seems like a lot. People are going to keep walking instead of buying them."

"I was thinking five dollars," says Kunal. He catches my eye. "How much are you and Maribel selling your pies for?"

"We aren't totally sure, but I think ten dollars," I say.

Gilbert lets out a low whistle. "That's really expensive. Most things at Avery Local are a lot lower."

"And besides," Victor says. "Are people going to carry around an entire pie with them while they're at the festival? That just seems complicated."

"I—I hadn't thought of that," I mumble, looking down at my desk. Maribel and I should have thought of this before. We've been so excited to find a recipe and make them, we really hadn't thought about the logistics of people buying them.

"Maybe you could sell it by the slice," Drew says.

"Super messy," Gilbert points out. "Plus you'll have to cut each piece and how do you make it even?"

Kunal snaps his fingers. "Wait a minute, how about making little individual pies?"

Victor nods. "Maybe people would buy even more that way."

"It might be more work," I say.

Gilbert shrugs. "Maybe a little bit more. But think about it—a family might come to your booth and buy one pie for ten dollars. But what if a family comes to your booth with three kids? If they buy one for each kid at five dollars a pie, that's fifteen dollars. Maybe more if the parents want one too."

"That's a really good idea," I say. I take out a pen and write Mini Pies on my hand so I don't forget to tell Maribel.

Meanwhile, the group keeps talking about their pricing. They're stuck on how much to charge. Drew and Kunal want to charge five dollars, while Gilbert and Victor want to charge four. It seems like a small difference, but as the discussion goes on, both sides just get madder.

"Hey," I say. "What if you sell little cotton balls for kids to launch? You could sell it separately or bundle it with the catapult for an extra dollar or something."

Gilbert and Drew exchange glances.

"That could work," says Kunal. "Or maybe, those little craft things, what are they called—pom-poms?"

"You could get black ones and call them cannonballs," I say. "Like in *Kingdom of Krull*."

I may not play the game, but I've seen enough online videos to at least know that.

Drew's face brightens. "Now *that* is a good idea."

Kunal claps me on the shoulder. "Thanks, Elliott."

I keep my smile casual, but on the inside I feel triumphant. I'm not in their project, but at least one of my ideas is.

CHAPTER 31

It's the day before the festival. Maribel and I have one simple goal: to make pies until we collapse.

After school, we head to the pickup line. I readjust my backpack—it's stuffed full of everything I'll need this weekend. After I finish baking at Maribel's, I'm going to Dad and Kate's. Dad actually was able to rearrange his schedule, so he should be back in town tomorrow afternoon, just in time to swing by the festival. Normally, I wouldn't go over to their place if Dad was out of town. But he asked me to keep an eye on her, and besides, I'm starting to think Kate is pretty okay. When I told her I'd bring her a freshly baked pie for dinner tonight, she sighed and said that would be absolutely perfect.

"I did a practice run with the mini pie tins," Maribel says as we walk. "They take a little less time in the oven, so that's good. We have a lot of pies to make!"

When I told her Kunal's idea, she was just as excited as I thought she'd be. She found a local place that carried the little tins, so we're all set for making our pies tonight.

Maribel's dad, Gabriel, picks us up, and soon we are in the kitchen preparing our ingredients. We melt butter in a big pot on the stove, crack eggs in an enormous stainless steel bowl, and have vinegar and vanilla premeasured and ready to go.

We make an assembly line. First, I pat the crust into the pie pans, and then Maribel adds the filling. We put the little pies on cookie sheets and slide one batch after another into the big oven. When the pies come out, we grate fresh nutmeg on top. I found that idea in a recipe online, and it turned out to be the perfect thing—a bit of a splurge, but it adds a just-right amount of sharpness to what might be an almost too-sweet pie.

Outside, the sky begins to darken. The doorbell rings, and Maribel's mom answers it. When she returns, she's carrying two large pizza boxes. My stomach rumbles.

"Surprise," Carla says.

Maribel and I grin. I've never been happier to see pizza.

Carla calls upstairs to Gabriel, who joins us in the kitchen. The four of us eat standing up around the kitchen island, eating our slices. One pizza is spinach-ricotta and the other is pineapple, pepperoni, and olive. Both are delicious.

"I cried every night until we found a good gluten-free pizza place," Maribel says.

"And *I* cry every time you order pineapple pizza," Maribel's dad jokes.

"Dad!" Maribel says, but she's laughing and so am I. Pineapple pizza is *good*. I don't know why the older generation can't appreciate that.

I like talking with Maribel and her family. She's already told them how much I like cooking and how I'm using the project to raise money for culinary camp. Gabriel asks me some questions about cooking, and I can tell he really listens to what I have to say. "So, Elliott," Carla says. "Maribel says your brother is coming soon, is that right?"

Maribel turns sideways so I can see her gross-out face.

I hide my laugh into a slice of pizza. "Four more weeks."

Gabriel's eyes twinkle. "I miss those baby days. I'd go back and do it all over again in a heartbeat."

Carla grins. "Those days were lovely—exhausting, but lovely! And of course it helped that Maribel was the sweetest, most serious little baby."

Jokingly, I widen my eyes, pretending like I'm shocked to hear this. "Maribel, serious? Gee, I can't imagine that."

Her parents crack up.

Gabriel points his pizza crust at Maribel. "He got you there."

"Hey!" Maribel says. "I'm not that serious!"

"Yes, you definitely are," Gabriel says. "We love you for it though."

Carla turns to me. "When Maribel was little she was *beyond* adorable—with the softest, roundest cheeks and huge brown eyes. But she wasn't a pushover. People tried to squeeze her, but then she would pipe up with a big, strong voice, saying, 'No, thank you!'"

Gabriel beams. "I always loved that. Her parents and her big brother and sister wanted to baby her, but she was always her own person."

Maribel's cheeks redden. "Mom, Dad. This is so embarrassing."

Gabriel and Carla pull out their phones and start scrolling. They're both searching for the ultimate Maribel baby picture, I guess. Maribel is covering her eyes with her hands. I try not to laugh, but it is so funny seeing Maribel act embarrassed like this.

Gabriel wins the photo-finding contest and shows me a picture of little Maribel. She is wearing a blue raincoat and boots and holding a striped umbrella.

I don't really know what to say, so I just nod.

Maribel winces. "Are we done? Elliott and I need to get back to work."

"That's our Maribel," Gabriel says. "You can always trust her to keep a train moving in the right direction."

Maribel laughs it off, but I wonder if she hears the pride in his voice. Maribel's dad seems to really see who she is. Carla too. I know she thinks they're disappointed in her for not wanting to be a doctor, but all I can see is how much they love her. It's like they keep their love really close to the surface—so close to the surface that it might bubble over at any time.

I wish that's how Dad was with me.

It was nice, the way Maribel's parents talked about her as a baby. And speaking of babies, it's hard to believe that Dad and Kate will have one soon. Even though Kate's stomach keeps getting bigger—and her book keeps mentioning larger and larger vegetables—it doesn't seem quite real. For some reason, it's easier to think of the baby as a romaine lettuce than as an actual, real, almost-here *baby*.

We get to work, making pie after pie. When we finish, we are a tired, sticky, mess—but we're also happy.

We load into Maribel's mom's car. While she drives me to Dad and Kate's, Maribel reviews the details for tomorrow.

"We'll pick you up early, and we'll have a couple boxes of pies," she reminds me. "And then later on in the morning, my parents will bring more pies to replenish the ones we will have hopefully sold by then."

"Hopefully," I echo.

Maribel punches me in the arm lightly. "*Definitely* is what I meant. The ones we will have *definitely* sold by then."

They drop me in front of Dad and Kate's.

I open the front door and then turn around to wave goodbye. "Thank you for the ride!" I yell. Their car backs down the driveway and disappears into the night.

I step inside and close the door behind me. "Kate, I'm back!"

There's no answer.

"Kate! I'm here!" I say again, louder this time. "I brought you a pie!"

"Elliott?" Kate's voice sounds groggy.

I go to the family room. Kate is lying on the sofa. She tries to sit up when I come in, but she's moving very slowly. It isn't very Kate-like at all.

"Are you okay?" I ask.

She tries to smile. "I'm seeing spots and I have a headache—I'm probably just overtired. It's nothing."

My stomach squeezes. "That doesn't sound exactly normal."

"It's been a weird day," Kate admits. "Today I tried to put on my shoes and they wouldn't fit. I had to get my flip-flops out of the closet."

With some effort, she puts her feet up on the coffee table. They don't look normal. They're swollen and tight. The truth is, they don't even look like human feet. They look ogre-sized.

I bite my lip. "I think we should call Dad."

Kate pulls her sweater around her. She stays still like that for a long time. I think she's going to tell me not to worry.

"Okay," she says quietly. "Maybe you're right."

CHAPTER 32

I call Dad, but it goes straight to voice mail.

"I just remembered—he's giving that speech." Kate sighs. "He probably can't check his phone right now. Just text him—he'll call when he can."

Dad is in Washington, DC—which is at least an hour away by plane and way more by car. What is he going to do from that distance? If I wait around for him, things could get worse for Kate. And for the baby.

The back of my neck prickles. I have to do something. I pick up my phone and video-call Mom, but it goes straight to voice mail. I call again. This time she answers.

"Hi, Elliott," Mom says. Through the screen, I can see she's somewhere crowded. A restaurant, I think.

"Mom?" I say. "Where are you?"

"Hold on," she says. "Let me get somewhere so I can hear you better."

I watch as she leaves the building and stands outside. There's still sounds of traffic and people going by, but it's much quieter.

"It's Kate—she has a bad headache and she's not feeling good." The words come out in a tangle.

Mom pauses. "Okay, Elliott. Take a deep breath."

I shake my head. "Mom, I don't need a deep breath! She has a huge headache, and she's seeing spots. Something's really wrong."

Mom wrinkles her forehead in concern. "Let me talk to her."

I pass the phone to Kate.

"Sorry to trouble you. Elliott was worried." Kate tries to sound cheerful, but her voice is shaking.

"It's okay," Mom says. "You're having a headache? What else is going on?"

"I'm seeing spots, but kind of silvery and blurred," Kate says. "And they're triangle shaped. It's really strange."

"Tell her about your feet," I interrupt. "Tell her they're swollen and huge, like ogre feet."

"I think you need to go to the hospital," Mom says.

Kate nods, then winces like it hurts even more. She hands me the phone.

Mom's not standing on the street anymore. She's inside

a parking garage, moving fast to her car—talking as she walks.

"Elliott, listen carefully. Help Kate get her shoes and purse. If she's already packed a hospital bag, take that too. I'm going to call a car to take her to the hospital. Go with her—she needs you."

I've never seen Mom look so serious. She disconnects the call.

Kate lets out a low groan.

I look at her. "Mom said you might have already packed a hospital bag?"

She closes her eyes. "It's on our dresser, blue bag with a shoulder strap."

I take the steps two at a time and run to Dad and Kate's room. It's right where she said it would be.

When I come downstairs, Kate's trying to slide her feet into flip-flops. Between the size of her feet and the fact that she can't bend over, it's not going very well.

"Here," I say. I bend over and help her put them on.

A car swings into the driveway. I hold Kate's elbow, and we head to the front door. At the last minute, I see one of her scarves hanging over the back of the chair, so I grab it. I don't want Kate to be cold at the hospital.

"Thanks, Elliott," she says.

I help Kate, and then slide in next to her. The driver is pretty fast, like maybe he is afraid the baby is going to get born right here in the back seat. Every time we go around a corner, Kate winces and rubs her stomach. She dials her doctor to let her know that we are going in.

Then Dad calls. Even through the phone, I can hear the worry in his voice and it makes everything feel more urgent somehow.

"He'll be on the next flight," Kate says.

I do the math in my head. An hour flight, plus travel to and from the airports. It could be a while.

We're zipping through the roads—everything feels quiet and urgent. We zoom past the rocket slide, then turn left at the purple house, but still it doesn't seem fast enough.

When we get to the hospital, the driver needs help knowing where to go. There are so many signs! Kate points out Labor & Delivery.

It honestly is not the best name—I mean, *labor* means work and *delivery* makes it sound like it has to do with packages. They should have called it "Babytown" or something a little nicer, but we eventually get to where we need to go.

I help Kate walk inside. She moves slowly in her flip-flops. The hallway is long, and there's a plasticky, hospital-y smell. A nurse wearing a pink shirt asks Kate a bunch of questions. She checks Kate's feet and takes her blood pressure—that's when things start to feel really serious.

"Preeclampsia," the nurse mutters.

"What is it?" I ask. "Is she going to be okay? What about the baby?"

The nurse points at me. "You're too young to go back

with her. Grab a seat in the waiting area—we'll come update you when we can."

"But she's by herself," I say. "Someone needs to stay with her."

Kate squeezes my hand. "It's okay, Elliott."

I want to believe her, but her voice is unsteady. Her eyes are turned down with worry. Other nurses have appeared out of nowhere. They make Kate sit in a wheelchair and take her away. One escorts me to the waiting area. The doors close behind me with a *whoosh*.

A feeling bubbles inside me. I think of Dr. Gilmore's wall. Mad, Sad, Brave, Calm. I'm none of these.

What I am is *scared*.

It's not a new feeling. For a long time now, I've been scared about the baby coming. Scared that there wouldn't be enough time for me. Scared that he would take my place. And most of all, scared that Dad would love him more. But now I'm *scared about the baby* in a completely different way.

I used to think that the baby was just another thing that would never feel like mine.

But the truth is, sometimes you don't really understand that something is yours until it seems like it might get taken away.

No matter what I said, no matter what I thought—no matter what I *did*—he is my brother.

Please let him be okay.

CHAPTER 33

The waiting room is a big area with lots of chairs and sofas. On one wall, there's a television showing *Binky Bunnies*—luckily, the sound is muted.

A huge crowd takes up one whole corner of the room. Everyone is talking and laughing—it's one giant family waiting for their newest addition to be born. Some are grandparent-age and some are parent-age and some are teenagers. There's a little kid asleep, his cheek pressed against a vinyl sofa. I wonder what it would feel like to be part of a big family like that—where everyone is together all the time and no one is ever split down the middle.

I sit on the quieter side of the room, a couple of rows away from two old men sitting together holding a bouquet of pink flowers and a little pink teddy bear. I don't feel like reading so I stare out the window.

And then I see her.

I jump to my feet. "Mom!"

She's walking so fast, it's almost a run. After she makes her way across the room, she gives me the biggest hug of my life.

I don't mind.

Eventually, we let go.

Mom takes a deep breath. "Come on. I saw a hot chocolate machine around the corner."

We walk down the hall, and Mom swipes her card. First my cup fills with hot cocoa. Then her cup fills with a sputter of coffee.

I take a sip. There isn't much of a chocolate flavor—it's more chocolate-ish. But it's comforting in that way that sweet, hot things can be.

Mom drinks from her cup. "Mmm. Hospital coffee—gotta love it." She says it in the way where she means the opposite.

"What is preeclampsia?" I ask. The name makes me think of things clamping down, which sounds painful.

"It's something that can happen in pregnancy," Mom says. "It has to do with high blood pressure—it can be bad for the mom and the baby."

"*Bad*? What does that mean?" I ask.

"It can be serious," Mom says. "But Kate is here. She has excellent doctors and nurses, and they'll watch closely to make sure her blood pressure goes down."

I gulp. "What if it doesn't?"

Mom sips her coffee before answering. "They might help the baby be born earlier."

"But he's not a watermelon yet!" I say.

Mom widens her eyes. "He's not a *what*?"

I explain to her about *Week by Week: Grown with Love.*

"He was a cantaloupe last week but is a romaine lettuce this week," I tell her.

Her eyes narrow. "But that doesn't make any sense. Cantaloupes are much heavier than lettuce."

I laugh. "That's exactly what Kate and I said!"

At first, I smile, remembering our watermelon walk around the kitchen, but then I get quiet. What if something goes really wrong and the baby never gets to be a watermelon? Tears pop into my eyes, and I wipe at them with the back of my hand. This feels like a different kind of crying than my good old Tear Tank. It's not an overwhelmed kind of crying.

Mom sees that I'm getting upset. She pulls on my arm. "Come on, let's go back to the waiting area. I saw some ancient magazines we can read to pass the time."

It's not the best offer, but at least it's something. We sit together, and I alternate between staring out the window and watching the other people in the waiting room.

Mom finishes her coffee. She tosses it into a nearby trash can. There's something different about her. I look at her closely to figure it out—like a live, in-person Spot the

Difference activity page. But it's not just one thing that's different. She did something to her hair to make it look straight and smooth. She's wearing a dress, which is not like Mom at all. And her face looks different too.

I squint at her. "Mom. Are you wearing *makeup*?"

I'm almost expecting her to say that it's a trick of the light, or maybe make a joke or something, but she just smiles.

"Yes," she says. "I am."

"Oh." The back of my neck gets warm. I don't know why I feel embarrassed, but I do. "What were you doing when I called you?"

"I was out with a friend," she says.

I trace the side of the hot chocolate cup, which has little dancing coffee beans on it.

"We never talk about what you do when I'm not with you," I say.

She nods. "Do you have some questions?"

I drink the rest of my cocoa, which is still not very chocolaty, and now it's not very hot either. I pull the lid off and start bending it back and forth. Little drips of chocolate get on my hands and shirt, but Mom doesn't say anything.

I clear my throat. "Are you going on dates and stuff?"

"Sometimes," Mom says.

"Oh," I say. But it feels more like: OH. Or maybe even *uh-oh*.

I twist the lid until it snaps. Then I start pulling apart the plastic into little shards. I drop them in my empty cup, and they make satisfying plinking sounds as they land.

"Elliott," Mom says softly. She reaches over and taps me gently on the head one, two, three times. "What's going on in there?"

"I don't want you to get married again." I blurt the words out.

"Well," Mom says gently. "It's not really up to you. But for the record, I don't want that either."

I look at her carefully. She's looking back at me. "Really? You don't?"

The side of her mouth turns up. "Does that surprise you?"

"I guess," I say slowly. "I thought maybe you were lonely and sad by yourself when I went to Dad and Kate's. Like, maybe it wasn't fair that Dad got married again."

Mom raises her eyebrows. "Not fair to who? To me?"

I nod. "It feels kind of uneven. Dad and Kate have each other—and the baby too, I guess. But you are alone."

She turns sideways in her seat. "The thing is, Elliott, *alone* and *lonely* are two different things. You can be lonely even if you're with other people."

All of a sudden, I think of my lunch friends. Sometimes when I sat with them, I would feel alone even though we were all together. I felt that way when they would talk about *Kingdom of Krull* and soccer. And then I really felt that way after they cut me out of their group.

That's not how I feel when I'm with Maribel. That's also not how I've felt when I've talked to Kunal on my own, away from the group.

"Sometimes I'm alone, but I'm not usually lonely," she continues. "I like being by myself. And I like being with people too. When you're away, I do both. You don't have to worry about me."

Tears pop into my eyes. "This year, with Malcolm gone, I felt alone and lonely."

Mom squeezes my shoulder. "It's been a tough year—one with lots of changes."

I take off my glasses and rub them on my shirt. "You know something? I used to be kind of mad at Kate. Because I already have you. I don't need an extra mom."

"You definitely have me," Mom says. "But."

I put my glasses back on. "But what?"

"But it's okay to have Kate too. We're both a part of your family," she says. "You can have us both."

I let out a deep breath I didn't know I was holding. "Really?"

She nods. "Having more people in your life who love you is a good thing. Like Kate. And the baby."

"But," I say, and then the Tear Tank goes into overdrive. I start crying fat, choking tears—the kind that launch out of my eyes and stick to my glasses, blotching them up.

She pulls me into a sideways hug. With the other hand, she searches in her purse until she finds a package of tissues.

I take one and blow my nose loudly.

"The thing is," I say. "I want a family like *that*."

Mom follows my glance and sees that I'm looking at the big family across the waiting area.

"I'm sure they have a lot of fun together," Mom says.

I nod, imagining birthdays and epic family vacations. Inside jokes and traditions and big dinners with lots of food.

"I bet they do," I say.

"But all families have hard times," Mom says. "Everyone has struggles."

Two of the teenagers are playing that game where you try to slap the other person's hands. They keep missing because they are both cracking up. The little kid is now awake and being held by one of the grandma types. She's talking to him quietly and rubbing his back.

"I don't know," I say. "It looks pretty good from here."

"Just remember," Mom says. "Every family has good and bad. Theirs does—and yours does too. You can't compare your insides to someone else's outsides."

I close my eyes for a minute and think about the good things. Mom. Dad and Kate. Denver and Omelet. And the baby too. No one would know those good things just by looking at me.

Something aches deep in my chest.

"Mom," I say slowly. "I was so mad when Dad and Kate told me about the baby. What if that made Kate feel stressed? Maybe it hurt the baby. What if she's in the hospital because of me?"

Mom's eyes soften. "Oh, Elliott. Feelings don't cause bad things to happen."

"But I broke that window," I whisper. "It was such a bad thing."

Mom squeezes my shoulders. "You know, we've never talked much about what happened. I'd like to hear what you were feeling."

For the second time tonight, I think of Dr. Gilmore's wall: Mad, Sad, Brave, Calm.

I crumple my cup.

"This whole time, I thought I was just mad. And part of me *was* mad—Dad and Kate acted like I was supposed to do a cartwheel with happiness."

Mom rubs my back. I take a deep breath. "Also, I was sad because it felt like the family with you, me, and Dad was really done in a forever kind of way."

She nods. "Dad and I will always be connected because of you, but I understand what you're saying."

I swallow. "But even though I was mad and sad, I never realized how scared I was. Not until tonight."

Mom squeezes my hand. "Scared?"

My cheeks get warm. "I'm sorry—I know it's selfish to talk about that now, with the preeclampsia and everything— but I was so scared that the baby would take my place."

At first, I think Mom's going to say something like "you could never be replaced," but instead she squeezes harder.

"Did I ever tell you about what happened when Uncle Greg was born?" she asks.

I shake my head. Uncle Greg lives in Maine. Mom and I visited him last summer and ate our weight in lobster.

"I was five years old," Mom says. "He'd just come home from the hospital, and of course your grandma was taking care of him all the time—you know, babies take a lot of time. A *lot*!"

I nod, even though I don't really. I guess I will soon enough.

"My hair was so long back then," she continues. "I could sit on it. Grandma would brush it out and braid it after my bath. You've seen old pictures at her house—do you remember the one where I'm wearing the strawberry dress?"

In my head I can see it: Mom as a girl with long, blond braids. "I think so."

She nods. "So, Baby Uncle Greg was probably nursing, and Grandma thought I was off playing with my dolls, but I wasn't. Instead, I sneaked upstairs to their bedroom and got the sharp scissors out of her sewing box."

My eyes widen. This sounds dangerous. *"And?"*

Mom's eyes twinkle. "Then I climbed onto the bathroom counter and cut my hair off—every single strand."

My eyes widen. "What? You were bald?"

She laughs. "Not *bald*, exactly—but close. There was hair *everywhere*."

"What happened after that?"

"Well, Grandma eventually wondered what had happened to me. When she found me, she yelled at me and then she cried. And then *I* cried. Then we both cried, together, sitting on the pink tile floor with piles of hair all around us."

Mom has a far-off look in her eyes. "You aren't the first one to have a hard time with a new sibling. Babies change a lot of things when they come. And before you know all the good things that come with a baby brother, it's easy to get a little stuck imagining the bad things. But it didn't take long before I really, really, loved your uncle Greg. I think it might be like that for you too."

She squeezes my hand, and I squeeze back.

"About the window," she says. "I don't want you to do it again. It was definitely not the right thing to do."

"Definitely not," I say.

"But part of me wonders if you were showing us that you needed help."

I open my mouth to answer, but then it somehow turns into a yawn.

"Maybe," I say finally.

"Tired, huh?" she asks.

"A little," I say. "Maribel and I made a bazillion pies today."

Mom pats her shoulder. "If you want to close your eyes, you can put your head here."

If we were anywhere else, I would probably say no. But it seems like a hospital waiting room is a place where it's okay to do lots of things. So I lean against her and we look out the window like that. The view is just office buildings, but there's a little grassy courtyard down below and someone has wrapped the trees in twinkle lights.

I think about whoever did that—whoever thought that it would be nice to make those trees pretty and if they knew that people in the waiting room might see.

I think about how we don't know about other people's insides.

I think about Mom cutting all her hair off when she was a little girl and how mad Grandma must have been.

And I think about Dad traveling hundreds of miles to get here soon, and I also think of Mom, and Kate and the baby. How my family doesn't all live together or all have big parties together, but maybe my family is okay anyway. Not for any real reason in particular but just because it is mine.

CHAPTER 34

Elliott. *Elliott.*"

It's Mom's voice. She's patting my arm gently, helping me wake up. But when I open my eyes, the first person I see is Dad.

"Hey," he says. He's crouched down, at eye level with me. I'm still on Mom's shoulder.

I look around, blinking. "Is Kate okay? The baby?"

"I just checked on her," Dad says. "The nurses are keeping a very close watch, but we'll probably be here for a while. Mom's going to get you home so you can rest."

I scratch my head and adjust my glasses. I'm so tired that my brain feels fuzzy. "I'll stay here. I want to make sure that Kate and the baby are okay."

Dad shakes his head. "It might be days, Elliott. You have Avery Local tomorrow. I promise I'll keep you posted."

I rub my eyes. I'm too tired to think. My eyes want to close again. My body wants to be horizontal.

"Come on," Dad says. He holds out his hand and pulls me to standing. I think he's going to move aside, but instead he squeezes me in a hug.

This is the thing: Dad and I haven't hugged for a long time. I guess he thought I was too grown up for it. Or maybe I thought that.

Honestly, the hug is awkward. His arms aren't soft like Mom's. My head is jammed sideways against his collarbone. But I think it's okay, actually, hugging Dad. Maybe better than okay.

He pats my back. He waits until I let go.

"You did great, El. Really great." His voice is scratchy and—

What? No.

His eyes are *watering*.

Dad has a Tear Tank?

"Thanks for taking care of them," he says to Mom, and I'm not sure if he's talking about Kate, or the baby, or me. Maybe all of us.

"Of course," Mom says. Then he hugs her too.

He goes through the double doors to Kate and the baby.

Mom slings her purse over her shoulder. "Ready to go?"

I realize that the rest of the waiting area is empty.

"What happened to that big family? Did they have their baby?"

Mom smiles. "A little girl—eight pounds. You slept right through it."

We walk to the parking garage. As soon as we get home, I check on Denver and Omelet and then I go to bed. I'm pretty sure that I fall asleep even before my head hits the pillow. I dream about watermelon babies all night long.

CHAPTER 35

I wake up early and bounce out of bed. It's Avery Local Day!

And then I remember: Kate is in the hospital. I grab my phone and text Dad. He replies right away, saying that nothing has changed yet. He also wishes me good luck with the festival.

Mom is still sleeping. Last night, she arranged for Maribel's parents to pick me up here. I told her I would get ready by myself, and I do. I'm waiting outside on the front steps when Maribel and her dad pull up. In the back seat, Maribel holds a box of pies. The three-ring binder is on the seat next to her.

"What happened?" she asks. "Your mom told my parents that Kate had an emergency."

I explain everything that happened last night. The whole time, Maribel listens with huge, round eyes.

"Dad," she says. "Is Kate going to be okay? And the baby?"

I guess that's the good thing about having a doctor around—they know some of this medical stuff.

"It sounds like they caught it early," Gabriel says. "It's really good that Elliott got her to the hospital."

"What if Kate's blood pressure won't go down?" Maribel asks.

He glances in the rearview mirror at us. "Sometimes everyone is safer after the baby is delivered. Elliott might be a big brother soon."

I pat my sweatshirt pocket. "My dad said he would call me if anything changes."

Maribel elbows me. "Did you turn your ringer all the way up? Vibration too?"

I nod. "Believe me, I don't want to miss it."

At school, the parking lot is full of cars. Gabriel drops us off and tells us that he and Carla will come later with the rest of the pies.

We're carrying two pie boxes, the three-ring binder, plus the poster we need to attach to our booth. After we check in, we make our way outside to the field and start looking for our booth.

"What if no one likes our pies?" I ask.

She shakes her head. "Impossible. They're really good, and you know I wouldn't just say that. Remember how much my parents liked them too? Not to mention your mom's reaction last week."

We smile for a moment, remembering. But when we find our booth, Maribel's face clouds.

"I don't think we got a good location. People aren't going to come all the way out to the field when they could just do the loop inside the gym."

Now it's my turn to make her feel better. "No way. The day is going to be beautiful. Who'd want to be cooped up inside when they could be out here?"

Maribel chews her lip. "You think so?"

"I know so," I say. "Besides, this is where most of the food booths are. People will definitely make an effort to find us."

Maribel's glance flickers sideways, to where Parker and her crew are setting up their cupcake booth. Their signs look professional,[31] and they're also covered in glitter.[32] They're all wearing matching shirts[33] with cupcakes on them. Our sign is made with stick-on letters and smiling pies that Maribel drew. We didn't even think about coordinating our clothes.

"Don't worry about them," I say.

Maribel nods. "You're right. I need to focus."

I almost laugh—because the idea of *me* telling a laser

---

[31] Of course.
[32] Double of course.
[33] Triple of course!

beam like Maribel Martinez to focus is just beyond words. But sometimes I'm a laser beam about some things.

While we're attempting to tape our sign to the booth, my phone buzzes in my pocket. But it's just a text from Mom saying she's on her way.

Maribel looks up. "Any news?"

I shake my head. "Not yet." I feel jumpy, waiting for whatever's going to happen.

Ms. Choi walks by our booth. She's got a clipboard in her hands and is wearing a shirt that says Avery Local Staff.

"Hey there," she says. "Do you have everything you need?"

I hold up our tape roll. "This stuff is pretty useless. Would you have anything stronger?"

Ms. Choi rummages in her messenger bag and holds out a roll of duct tape. I peel some off, and she cuts it with scissors. We work together until the sign is secured. It may not be as flashy as Parker's sign, but it does the job.

"Looks good," Ms. Choi says.

Maribel holds up one of our mini pies. "Do you want to try one, Ms. Choi?"

Ms. Choi rubs her hands together. "I thought you'd never ask."

She hands some money to Maribel—Maribel tries to say that there's no charge, but Ms. Choi waves her off. Maribel tucks the money in our metal box, and we beam at each other. It's the first money that anyone's ever paid for our food, and it feels special—important. And it's extra nice that Ms. Choi is our first customer.

Ms. Choi takes a bite of pie. I hold my breath, waiting for her reaction.

A huge grin spreads across Ms. Choi's face. "This is *delicious*! What did you say is in this again?"

"Vinegar, sugar, and eggs," Maribel says, and smiles. "And Elliott's special crumble crust."

"Vinegar, huh? I was expecting some great things from this partnership, but this is beyond anything I could have pictured."

Ms. Choi takes another bite. And another, and another—until the pie is gone and we can see the shiny bottom of the foil pie plate. She wipes her mouth and folds her napkin into quarters.

"You might want to call Maribel's dad," she says. "I have a feeling you're going to need those extra pies."

CHAPTER 36

The gates open, and at first, we don't have a lot of visitors to our area.

"See?" Maribel hisses. "Where is everyone?"

I crane my neck. "People go through the gym first, and there's so much stuff to see there. But they'll show up—trust me."

She scoffs and starts rearranging the already perfectly placed pies.

I hope I'm right.

An hour goes by, and people start trickling onto the fields. The kettle corn booth is a big hit. I see a couple of kindergartners holding candy apples and marshmallow pops.

A little kid walks by with her own, personal *Kingdom of Krull* catapult—the project for the group I was almost a part of. I wait for the stab of jealousy, but it doesn't come. I don't like that I was left out, but they're still my friends. I'll visit those guys later. Besides, this project with Maribel worked out pretty well. If only someone would actually buy one of our pies.

I turn to Maribel. "Do you know what we need? Free samples!"

"Yes, that's a good idea!" She grabs a plastic knife and starts cutting a pie into bite-sized pieces. I put a fork in each piece so people can grab them.

"Free samples!" I yell.

"Excuse me, would you like a sample of some desperation pie?"

People start looking our way. A couple of families come over.

"What's desperation pie?"

Maribel grins like she's been waiting her whole life to explain our pies. She tells about going to Avery Market and discovering the community cookbooks and their desperation pies. Her face is animated, and she uses her hands to make big gestures. The crowd is mesmerized. And what's even better, they aren't just trying the samples— they're actually getting in line with money in their hands.

I make change as fast as I can. Some people buy one for now and an extra for later. A family with two grandparents, an uncle, and six kids comes through the line. They buy one for each person! Maribel just keeps handing out the pies and chatting with everyone.

The money box is filling up fast, but the best part is watching people eat the food we made.

A woman takes one bite and says "This is delicious!" She immediately gets back in line to buy a few more.

A kid cries because he is too full to eat anymore but says he wants to keep tasting it anyway.

An old man with tears in his eyes comes over to shake our hands. "This reminds me of a pie my mother made when I was a boy. Thank you for reminding me of home."

Soon, the pie boxes are almost empty.

"We're running low on stock," I tell Maribel as we fill an order for four pies.

She looks at her phone to check the time. "Mom and Dad should be here soon."

And just as she says the words, I see Maribel's parents and my mom coming through the crowd.

"Hi!" Mom says. "I got here just as Carla and Gabriel were unloading their car and figured they must be Maribel's parents."

Carla laughs. "Lucky you were there to help us carry these boxes."

Gabriel holds up his boxes. "Where should I put these? Can we help?"

"You've got quite a crowd," Mom says.

"It's all because of Maribel," I say. "If she doesn't end up running a big business someday, she could definitely go into sales. Or speech giving."

I say it loud enough so her parents can hear. They don't

say anything. But Carla smiles to herself. She's listening, at least.

The parents decide to go check out the other booths. Maribel and I keep selling our pies. Our line stretches all the way to Parker's cupcake booth. It looks like they're getting some customers too—but not as many as we are.

Ms. Choi comes by again—she's with Janiyah from Avery Market. She has a matching Avery Local Staff shirt and rainbow socks.

"Oh!" Maribel says when she sees them. "I'm glad you're here, Janiyah—we want to give you one of the pies."

"Oh, no," says Janiyah, taking out her wallet. "I'm happy to pay."

"We wouldn't have known about desperation pie if it weren't for you," Maribel says.

I nod. "We owe you."

Maribel turns to Ms. Choi. "Do you want another one, Ms. Choi?"

Ms. Choi hesitates, glancing at our pie box.

"Maybe I shouldn't—you're running low."

"Take it, it's okay," I say. I wish we'd made a hundred more.

Maribel scrunches up her forehead. "Would you have another clipboard we could borrow? I was thinking that if we collected contact information, we could let people know if we make them again."

Maribel catches my eye and grins.

I laugh. "You act like you're running a corporation already!"

She shrugs. "You know you love it."

She's right. I do.

Maribel grabs a green gel pen. At the top of the paper, she writes Desperation Pie Pop-Up Event Contact List.

I raise my eyebrows. "Now we're doing pop-up events?"

"Anything is possible," Maribel says.

And the thing about it is that I actually believe her.

Meanwhile, Janiyah is polishing off the pie. "This is *fantastic*. Good job, you two."

"Well," I say. "If Avery Market ever wants to sell historically accurate pies, you know where to look."

Janiyah taps her finger on her chin thoughtfully. "That's not a bad idea at all."

In my head, I suddenly see dollar signs. I know we've been working on a business project this whole time, but for some reason, I'd never thought about the fact that we might actually be able to make some serious money. That's something I'm going to have to share with Dad, the next time I see him.

Maribel elbows me. "Now who's running a corporation?"

"Me," I say. "Us."

Because Maribel isn't just my business partner. She's also my friend.

CHAPTER 37

After the pies are all sold out, we get lots of names on our contact list. Maribel counts the money—my half is almost five hundred dollars. It's not everything I need for the basement window, but it's close.

We decide to take turns walking around the festival.

I buy a big bag of kettle corn and wander from booth to booth, looking at everyone's projects. Besides the food sellers, there are other, more experimental-looking projects. One group of girls invented a sleeping bag that's made of a special material to reflect heat back into the bag. Another group tested out different kinds of materials for skateboard wheels to try to give a smoother ride.

Inside the gym is loud but fun. One booth is selling little

Clone of the Stars parachute action figures, so I buy an alien one for Dad—a subtle hint that he should respect them a bit more. I find a small ceramic pot for Mom and a hair clip for Kate. I look and look for the baby, and finally find a purple hat made with really soft material.

I see Mom and Maribel's parents over by an area selling hand-painted vases. They show me their purchases, and I tell them we sold all the pies.

"I can believe it," Mom says. "We bought a lot of things, but we all agree that nothing was as good as those pies you made."

I see Victor, Kunal, Drew, and Gilbert at their booth. They're busy, and the catapults are selling fast.

Kunal catches my eye. "Hey, Elliott. Do you want one?"

He tosses a catapult in my direction—miracle of miracles, I actually catch it.

I reach into my pocket for money, but he shakes his head.

"For free," he says. "Since there were four of us, we made so many of them. I think we're going to have a lot left over."

"All our pies sold out," I say.

He grins. "Really? That's great!"

"Your idea about selling mini pies was a good one. Sometimes families came by and bought a pie for each person," I say.

His face falls. "Oh no, I just realized that I'm not going to get to try one."

"Don't worry—we'll make more," I say. "Maybe some-time you could join us."

Kunal's cheeks flush. "With . . . Maribel Martinez?"

I grin. I remember when I thought of her as a two-name kind of person.

"You can just call her Maribel, you know. Unless you want me to start calling you Kunal Gouthama."

He shakes his head slowly, with a strange, dreamy look on his face. I just laugh.

Back at the booth. Maribel has gotten lots of sign-ups. She waits until no one is around and then turns to me, grinning.

"You'll never guess who put her name on our list."

She points at a name.

I try not to fall over. "*Kennedy* signed up?"

"She actually apologized," Maribel says. "She said she didn't really understand how serious the gluten-free thing is for me."

"I'm glad she said she was sorry," I say. "Because that was so messed up!"

"I'm glad too," Maribel says. "But is it weird that I'm also glad that she said what she did? If she hadn't, you and I would never have been partners. We wouldn't even know about desperation pie."

"I'm really glad too," I say. "I can't imagine my life with-out that pie."

Maribel smacks me in the arm.

I laugh. "Okay, and I'm also glad we were partners!"

Maribel rolls her eyes. "That's better! I'm going to go walk around—see if you can get some more names for our list."

I'm still grinning as she walks away. A few people come by and sign our sheet. I'm down to the remnants of my kettle corn when my phone buzzes. It's Dad requesting a video call.

"Hi, Dad," I say when his face comes into view.

"Hey, Elliott. How's the festival?"

"It's good—we sold out of our pies. How's Kate?"

He sighs. "She's feeling pretty rough. They're giving her medicine, but her blood pressure keeps spiking up."

Dad's face looks tired. He probably didn't sleep much last night.

"Tell her hi for me," I say. "And that I hope[34] she's okay."

Dad rubs at his eyes. "You know, Elliott—I'm really proud of you. You're good at looking out for people—just like you looked after Kate last night."

I shift uncomfortably. "Oh, I don't know, Dad. It was just obvious she wasn't feeling well."

Dad shakes his head. "Not just that—like how you always watch out for me and make sure I don't accidentally order cilantro. Or when you get pickles for Kate. You're

---

[34] I want there to be an even better word than *hope*. But that's all I've got.

really good at that kind of thing. I'm not always so good at it."

I shrug. "You're good at lots of things I'm terrible at. Like throwing a ball. Like being focused."

He sighs. "I've been thinking a lot these past few weeks—remembering when your mom and I were waiting for you to be born. I was so excited. I wanted to show you the right way to do everything."

The back of my neck starts to sweat. I'm pretty sure he's about to remind me that I'm not very good at learning from him. I definitely don't want to hear this over speakerphone while at Avery Local.

"Dad, can I switch you to a regular call?"

He nods. But this is the weird thing—right before I switch him over to a voice call, he's wiping at his eyes again, and . . . is Dad crying again?

"Okay," I say after we switch over.

"Yeah." Dad's voice is low and scratchy. I get myself ready to hear whatever he's going to say.

He takes a deep breath. "I remember the first time I held you. I prayed that nothing bad would ever happen to you. I wanted your life to be perfect. Easy."

"Life isn't supposed to be easy, Dad," I say.

"I know, it's just—seeing your kid go through struggles is awful. I think that's why I might be hard on you. I want you to be ready for whatever the world throws your way."

I think about what the world has thrown my way. The

Divorce. Malcolm moving. My lunch friends leaving me out of their group.

There are other things the world has thrown my way too. Mom and Dad. Kate too. Friends to have lunch with. Better friends, like Maribel and Kunal. Teachers like Ms. Choi. Denver and Omelet, the cutest guinea pigs in the world.

I blow out a deep breath. "I think I'm ready, Dad. I think I'm doing okay."

And then I hear Dad make a snuffling sound, and now I *know* he is crying—and part of me feels like I might cry too, even though I'm happier than I've been in a long time.

"Yeah, El. You're doing okay. You're doing better than okay."

CHAPTER 38

Today I get to meet my baby brother. His name is Jonah.

Two nights ago, Dad called right before I went to bed. The doctors had spent enough time watching Kate's blood pressure level off, only to pop up again. They decided to help Jonah come earlier.

I couldn't see him right after he was born. Kate was still feeling sick, and the doctors needed to keep an eye on Jonah to make sure he was breathing okay. Dad sent me a few pictures though. Mom and Maribel said he was cute, but the truth is that he looked just like every other newborn baby, all squinchy and wrinkled.

But today they're ready to see me, so Dad picked me up early this morning. We made a quick stop at Sugar Rose for two big boxes of doughnuts—one for us and one for the nurses. Dad ordered iced coffee for Kate, but I'm the one who remembered that she likes it half-decaf with a single pump of hazelnut syrup.

While we're waiting for the coffee and doughnuts to be boxed up, Dad turns to me. "So, I want to tell you something. It's not a secret, but I also haven't found a good time to discuss it. And I guess I realized that sometimes there isn't a good time, but I should bring it up anyway. Because when we don't keep talking, that's when it gets harder to find each other."

I look at him sideways. "I honestly have no idea what you mean."

He clears his throat. "So, that time I bumped into you at Dr. Gilmore's office? That's because I've actually been seeing a therapist there."

My eyes get big. "*That's* the person I saw you with?"

Dad nods. "I started going a few months ago. Elliott, you probably don't know this, but I feel responsible for the way you struggled with schoolwork earlier this year. I should have known that transitioning to sixth grade would be a big deal. I wish I'd been able to support you more."

I blink, taking in his words. "I—I didn't know you felt that way."

The corner of his mouth quirks up. "It turns out, I'm not that good at talking about my feelings. But I want to do better—for you and for Jonah. For Kate. And I guess for me too."

When Dad says this, my mind basically explodes.[35]

Dad claps me on the shoulder in a kind of manly way. But then he turns it into a hug, right there in the middle of the doughnut shop.

I guess you could say he's trying. I guess you could say that I am too.

It looks different inside the hospital. At night, it was dim and almost unreal, but now everything is crisp and sharp. We walk past the waiting area, but today it's empty. At the check-in desk, they snap a plastic bracelet on my wrist with Jonah's name on it. After that, the double doors swing wide.

I follow Dad down the hall. There are whiteboards by each of the rooms, and we head for the one that says Sawyer and "It's a Boy!"

When we step inside, Kate is sitting up in bed. Dad had warned me in the car that she still looked pretty swollen. She does—but even so, she looks a *lot* better than she did that night we came in. She's holding the baby, who is wrapped up like a burrito. He has a knit hat on his head, and between that and the blanket, I can't really see his face.

"Have a seat," Dad says. He puts a pillow in my lap.

There are all kinds of instructions.

---

[35] Not literally. But almost.

"Place your arms like this. Keep your hands here so you support his head," he says.

I wipe my sweaty palms on my shorts. I'm not sure I want to hold him. What if I do it wrong? What if I hurt him?

Before I know it, Dad is handing me the warm little bundle. Jonah is so light, it's like holding a feather. It's almost like holding nothing at all.

But then I look at his face, and I realize that's not right. Because Jonah is looking at me.

Holding Jonah is not like holding nothing. It's like holding *everything*.

Kate wraps herself in her sweater. "Isn't he wonderful?"

His chin is smaller than my thumb. His eyes are blue and serious. His skin is just like a peach, soft and dusted with a light fuzz that glints golden in the light. *This is Jonah. This is my brother.*

"He's awesome," I whisper.

Kate grins at me—a new kind of smile.

"I didn't know that babies came this small," I say. I think of Kate's book. He's definitely not a melon or a pumpkin.

"Remember, he was early," Dad says. "A little smaller than they usually are."

I can't stop looking at Jonah. "He's good though, right? Strong and everything?"

"He's perfect," Kate says simply. "Just like his brother."

Something in her voice starts the Tear Tank. My eyes get wet, but for whatever reason, I don't even feel like I have to hide it. Before this exact moment, I never knew how important babies were. It feels like galaxies are swirling inside me. It feels like the gravity of the universe just shifted.

"Hi, Jonah," I say softly. "Hi."

His blanket has loosened, and one of his hands is up by his face. His fingers are impossibly delicate, so tiny and scrunched. Dad's going to be handing him a baseball before he can even walk—I just know it. But I'll be there too. I'll be handing him a whisk. I'll be learning his favorite recipes by heart.

As if he knows I'm thinking about food, he turns his head and makes a little squawking noise. His mouth opens like a baby bird looking for a worm.

"Okay, big brother," Dad says. "I think we need to get Jonah to his mom."

Dad takes him from me, and my arms feel empty. He rewraps Jonah and makes him into a snug burrito again. Kate sits up straighter in bed and arranges a circular pillow.

My cheeks burn. I panic for a moment, not sure what to do—should I leave? cover my eyes?—but she just rearranges some layers of her sweater and Jonah attaches with a little wet sound. If I didn't know he was nursing, I wouldn't have the slightest idea.

Kate pulls off his hat gently. She catches my eye and smiles. "If he's too cozy, he falls asleep. We want him to stay awake and eat."

"Eating is important," I say.

We're quiet for a moment, like that—just the sound of Jonah making little squeaks and baby grunts. The window looks out onto the highway where hundreds of cars are flowing past. I want to tell them: *Hey, my brother is here.*

Dad clears his throat. "So, we never circled back to that conversation about Jonah's middle name."

That's right—they wanted to give him a family name. Jonah will have Quigley as a middle name, just like me and Dad. I still feel tender at the thought. That was something that Dad and I had, just the two of us—our secret handshake. But if there's one person I don't mind sharing with, it's Jonah.

"It's okay," I say. "Quigley, right? Jonah Quigley Sawyer, like Dad and me?"

Kate and Dad exchange glances.

Dad's forehead creases. "Actually—no."

I frown, puzzled. *No?*

"We want to give him a family name," Dad continues. "But the Sawyer tradition is that *Quigley* is for the firstborn. That's you, Elliott. No one is replacing you. No one ever could."

I swallow hard, still not understanding.

Kate smooths Jonah's hair. "The trick was finding a family name that was just as special—just as important."

"Elliott," Dad says.

The syllables aren't full of disappointment—they're full of warmth. Of love.

"Yeah?" I ask.

Kate smiles, looking up. "If it's okay with you, we'd like to call him Jonah Elliott. After his brother."

I look at Kate and Dad. And then I look at Jonah. A family name—*my* name?

"We realized that we didn't have to look very far to find something special and important," Dad says. "It was right there in front of us the whole time."

And then Dad is hugging me, and I'm saying "okay" and we're both crying and so is Kate and if there's one thing I've learned since meeting Jonah it's that babies can sometimes cause Tear Tanks to overflow—they make the feelings leak out of your eyes like crazy—but no one seems to mind very much. In fact, that's maybe one of the best things about babies, if you want to know the truth.

CHAPTER 39

Mom!" I yell. "We're going to need a bigger refrigerator!"

"No, we don't!" Mom calls from down the hall. "It's not our fridge's fault that you're cooking for two events in one weekend."

I guess you could say that some things have changed in the weeks since Jonah was born.

Tomorrow, at Dad and Kate's, we're having a little party for Jonah—just the four of us. He's still little, so he can't eat yet, but it seemed like we should celebrate the day he was supposed to be born on. So we are calling it his Watermelon Day, because that's what Kate's baby book said for 40 weeks. Jonah may not have made it to watermelon size on the inside, but he's growing fast. Kate got him a watermelon onesie and hat, so he's going to wear that while Dad, Kate, and I eat. I planned the whole menu, and we're going to have watermelon-feta salad and grilled watermelon steak[36] and of course watermelon pie for dessert.

So in Mom's refrigerator, I have all my ingredients in various states of prep. Kate's become a lot more relaxed about me cooking in her kitchen—she says as long as someone is going to feed her, she won't say a peep. But I don't want to push it. And besides, sometimes it's tricky to cook when Jonah is around. Whenever I visit he wants me to hold him all the time. The truth is, I don't mind one bit.

The other half of the fridge is filled with stuff we're having for tonight's dinner at Mom's—sesame tofu, salmon, asparagus, and quinoa salad. Maribel and her parents are coming over and so are Kunal and his parents. Right after the festival, Kunal took me up on that invitation to make pies with Maribel and me. It turns out that we all get along and our families do too. Like Dr. Gilmore says, some friends are *talking* friends and some friends are more *doing* friends. But the best kinds of friends are both.

Tonight I'm cooking for a crowd, just like the title of that old Griffin Connor cookbook. I still think he's a genius, but I've decided that recipes can be a good thing. Life is confusing enough, so sometimes it's good to get actual instructions when you can.

---

[36] This is a real thing. I found it on the internet.

My phone rings, and it's Dad.

"Elliott," Dad says. "Do you think you might jump online later so we can try to defeat the Wayward Beast? I think we're getting really close."

No one could have ever predicted that Dad and Mom would let me get *Kingdom of Krull* and that Dad would decide to buy his own copy. Some days, I think he likes it even more than I do.

"Not tonight," I tell him. "Maribel and Kunal are coming over. But we'll find some time to play this weekend, okay?"

"Okay, El. See you tomorrow."

He holds up the phone so I can hear Jonah gurgling, and then we say goodbye.

I don't want to give the impression that things are perfect with Dad. He still thinks that I need to work harder at school (sometimes true) and that I should keep an open mind about sports (not a chance). But when I showed him all the pie money, he was really impressed. He said he didn't want the money for the window—he just wanted to make sure that I learned to be responsible for my mistakes. He hasn't officially changed his mind about cooking as a career, but he did tell me I should save that six hundred dollars for culinary camp. After he tastes the food I make at camp this summer, I hope he'll be even more open minded.

The kitchen timer beeps, and I pull out a fragrant, delicious desperation pie. I make one every time we get together, and no one ever gets tired of it. The truth is, there's something to be said for taking what you have and making the best of it.

Mom comes into the kitchen. She still hugs me a lot, and I still pretend that I mind.

"You're past my eyebrows now!" she exclaims.

I squirm away. "Mom, please. I'm sautéing the asparagus."

"Asparagus shamaragus," she says, which is so ridiculous I shouldn't laugh, but I do.

Mom starts clearing the counters, because she knows as well as I do that Kunal's and Maribel's families are going to bring a lot of food and we'll need space for it. She picks up some plants to temporarily relocate them.

"Mom," I say. "Leave the avocado where it is, okay?"

She hesitates. "You mean Imogene? Are you sure she won't be in the way?"

I nod. That little sprout sure has grown. Now it's a respectable houseplant in a pot with soil—it even has a stem and its very own leaves. It's made a lot of progress in a short amount of time. Even with all that progress, it can be hard to picture the big, strong tree it will become someday. But it deserves a place in the sun, and I'm cheering it on. Never underestimate the power of one person believing in you.

Then the front door is flying open and I hear Kunal's dad asking where he can put the dosas and Maribel asking where she can put the roasted beets and that means the night is officially beginning.

I used to wish for a big family. I didn't think what I had was enough. But recently, I've changed my mind about what the word *family* means. For me, it's Mom, Dad and Kate, and Baby Jonah of course. But it also means Maribel and Kunal and their families, and Malcolm and his moms too. There are a lot more people cheering me on than I ever realized. And, like Mom told me once—having lots of people to love you is a very good thing. Sometimes it's good to prepare for a crowd, because you never know exactly who's going to show up and be on your side. Which, when you think about it, is actually amazing.

As usual here in the kitchen, my brain is going in six hundred directions at once. One way is friends, and one way is family. One way is food, and one way is fun. One way is mistakes, and one way is progress. But the weird thing? Somehow, on a night like this, all these ideas point in the exact same direction—the one that says that honestly, we are here for each other. And together, we are all better than okay.

BABY BROTHER PIE

Surprising

Sweet

Sometimes
sticky

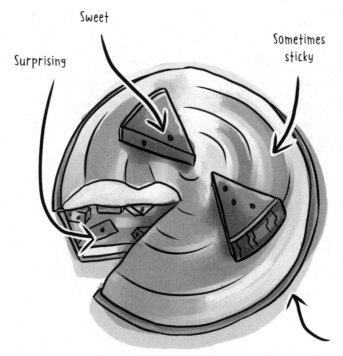

Worth it.

DESPERATION PIE

These recipes contain allergens such as dairy, eggs, and almonds. Please check for any allergies before preparing. Make with adult supervision.

INGREDIENTS:

One prepared piecrust
   (you can use your own recipe
   or use Elliott's, below)
4 large eggs
3 tablespoons apple
   cider vinegar

1 ¼ cups sugar
1 stick butter, melted
1 tablespoon vanilla
Optional: nutmeg, freshly
   grated

1. In a large bowl, beat together eggs, vinegar, sugar, melted butter, and vanilla, until the mixture is well combined.

2. Pour batter into prepared piecrust. Bake for 30 minutes at 425 degrees. Pie is done when center is set. Cool before serving.

ELLIOTT'S CRUMBLE CRUST

These recipes contain allergens such as dairy, eggs, and almonds. Please check for any allergies before preparing. Make with adult supervision.

INGREDIENTS:

¾ cup almond flour
1 tablespoon melted butter

3 tablespoons
powdered sugar

1. Preheat oven to 425 degrees for at least 20 minutes.
2. In a food processor, pulse ingredients until crumbly. (If you don't have a food processor, you can combine ingredients in a large bowl until clumps form.)
3. Press into and up the sides of an eight-inch pie plate or two mini pie tins. Bake for 15 minutes at 425 degrees until center is just set. Remove from oven and allow to cool before filling.

ACKNOWLEDGMENTS

I have a lot of people to thank, if you really want to know the truth.

Mary Kate Castellani, thank you for your enthusiasm for this project. You immediately understood where I wanted to go with it and you helped make the characters and story what they are today. Thank you for rolling with footnotes and recipes and pie art and the many different revisions that eventually led to Elliott finding his voice.

Marietta Zacker, thank you for reminding me that writing isn't supposed to be easy. Thanks to the entire team at Gallt & Zacker for all the support.

Brigid Kemmerer, I feel so lucky to have you as a friend and a writing partner. I appreciate every sprint, insightful comment, and hilarious text message, but most of all I appreciate your friendship.

Mirelle Ortega, your cover art is so wonderful. I still

haven't recovered from the cuteness of Denver and Omelet! Thank you for bringing these characters to life. Thank you to Marguerite Dabaie for the interior illustrations of Elliott's pies. I love them all but have to admit that Baby Brother Pie is my very favorite.

Thank you to the entire team at Bloomsbury Children's Books. I'm so thankful to work with all of you: Erica Barmash, Faye Bi, Nicholas Church, Laura Phillips, Phoebe Dyer, Beth Eller, Lex Higbee, Noella James, Jeanette Levy, Donna Mark, Jasmine Miranda, and Oona Patrick.

I was very fortunate to have several readers share their expertise with me—big thanks go to Alex Case, Laura Case, Alice Pierce, Sara Grochowski, Allie Haisty, and Christina Haisty for sharing their perspectives. Thank you to the Gluten Free Gang of Raleigh-Durham North Carolina for the insights about children's experiences with celiac disease. Extra special thanks to Korrin Ingalls, who was a wealth of knowledge and patiently answered my many questions about Kate and Jonah. Any mistakes are my own.

Thank you to the entire Springer family, and especially to Landon, who asked me to write a boy main character. Thank you to Kelli and Claire McDonald for always reading.

I'm lucky to have some of the best friends anyone could ask for. Gauri Johnston and Aislinn Estes—I don't know where I'd be without you. Caroline Flory, thank you for your wonderful insight, as always. Jackie and Dan Skahill, thank you for all the love and support. Anna Totten, Jess Redman,

Victoria Coe, Ashley Bernier, Wendy Chen, Mandy Hemingway, Mandy Roylance, Peter and Grace Flory, Lynne Kelly, Heather Clark, Cheryl Caldwell, Chris Baron, Jessica Kramer, Rajani LaRocca, Cory Leonardo, Josh Levy, Naomi Milliner, and Nicole Panteleakos, thank you for your friendship. Jared Turner, thank you for being my brother.

Nora, Leo, and Violet, what a year we had as this book was being written. Thank you for understanding what the sign on the door meant, thank you for checking in on me, thank you for all the hugs and encouragement. Thanks also to our dog Friday, who was always willing to go for a walk when I needed to think something out (and was equally willing to curl up at my feet while I wrote).

Jon, thank you for being there for me every step of the way—for this book, and in life in general. Honestly, I am so lucky to be married to you.